Jett was surprised
to see Glenna there

He studied her intently as she came into his room. "I wondered if he'd play his ace of hearts."

"You mean me?" Glenna frowned. "My father doesn't know I'm here. He wouldn't approve." Her eyes pleaded with him, then in a choked voice she went on, "Dad will lose not just the mine, but his home and everything. . . . There's no pride left in him, Jett. Please, help him."

"You don't know what you're asking, Glenna." Jett shook his head with an angry kind of weariness, his hands on his hips.

"Explain to me what I have to say or do to make you listen to me," she persisted.

"What if I told you to take off your robe?" His glance flicked to the satin bow with raw challenge.

And slowly Glenna raised a hand to untie the bow. . . .

JANET DAILEY AMERICANA

WILD AND WONDERFUL

Harlequin Books

TORONTO • NEW YORK • LONDON
AMSTERDAM • PARIS • SYDNEY • HAMBURG
STOCKHOLM • ATHENS • TOKYO • MILAN

The state flower depicted on the cover of this book is big rhododendron.

Janet Dailey Americana edition published May 1988
ISBN 373-89848-7

Harlequin Presents edition published March 1981

Original hardcover edition published in 1980
by Mills & Boon Limited

CHAPTER ONE

THE FIRE-RED PORSCHE convertible hugged the twisting, curving road through the West Virginia mountainscape, a splash of scarlet on the gray ribbon of concrete winding through the spring-green country. With the car's top down, the driver was exposed to the lingering sun and the billowing white clouds in the light blue sky.

Rounding a curve, Glenna Reynolds briefly lifted her face to the warmth of the sun. The teasing fingers of a speed-generated breeze tugged at her dark auburn hair, whirling its long curls away from her shoulders. A pair of owl-round sunglasses shielded her gray green eyes from the angling glare of the late afternoon sun. Contentment was etched in her vital and expressive features, a contentment born from a day spent pursuing journalistic pleasures.

On the passenger seat of the sports car, a camera was concealed in its leather case, along with a notebook containing scribbled impressions. Together the two contained a collection of springtime images that continued to float in Glenna's mind.

The wildly beautiful mountains and valleys of West Virginia had revealed its May treasures to her. Wildflowers were blooming at their peak, from the delicate lady's slipper to the flame azalea, their multicolored displays of beauty trapped in film. Jotted notations reaffirmed the camera's record of fox pups playing outside their den, tiny chipmunks darting about the forest floor, and the young fawn camouflaged and hidden at a meadow's edge.

Noted, too, were the sensations of being able to hear the new leaves growing, the fragile spring green rivaled only by the flowering red maple. Another time the hush of the woods had been broken by the drumming of a ruffed grouse. The camera shutter hadn't been quick enough to catch the jeweled flash of a scarlet tanager flitting through the trees, but hastily scribbled phrases had recorded the sighting on the pages of her notebook.

Captivated by the charm of spring, Glenn had tarried longer than she had intended. A glance at her watch increased the pressure of her foot on the accelerator pedal. The last thing she wanted was for her father to become concerned about her whereabouts. She regretted that she hadn't left him a message warning him that she might be late.

Since his heart attack this last winter, his second one, Orin Reynolds had become more conscious of her absences from him. Her father's attitude was not at all possessive. It was more an awareness of the shortness of his time to spend with her, something Glenna reciprocated in full. Even though he was as fully recovered from the attack as he would ever be, Glenna knew how slim the chance was that he would survive a third major attack.

She no longer took his presence in her life for granted and had adjusted her life-style and career to allow more time with her father. When he had been released from the hospital this last time, Glenna had wanted to give up everything to stay at home and take care of him. Orin Reynolds had rejected her suggestion, insisting that a temporary nurse and their housekeeper-cook, Hannah Burns, could take adequate care of him, and wisely informing her that she would need to escape into her writing. His advice had proved over and over again to be correct. If she needed further proof of it, the exhilarating flow of thoughts and ideas from today's outing provided it.

Braking, Glenna slowed the car to make the turn onto the graveled lane leading to the large white house nestled on the mountain slope amid the trees. It was a graceful old building, once the main house of a large estate, but the fertile valley land had been sold off some years ago. All that remained of the former land was the immediate grounds of the house and the few nontillable acres surrounding it.

Glenna recognized the car parked in the drive-way and smiled wryly. Although the doctor had limited the amount of time Orin Reynolds was allowed to spend at the office of his coal-mining operation to three days a week, her father had insisted on daily reports when he wasn't there.

Hence, Bruce Hawkins's car was a familiar sight.

The garage was separate from the house, a small stable converted some sixty years ago to hold automobiles. Its double set of doors beckoned to the red Porsche, but Glenna stopped the car short of its protection. There was time enough later to put it away.

Tipping her sunglasses atop her head, she collected the camera case and notebook from the passenger seat and left the car keys in the ignition for the time being. Her long legs swiftly climbed the veranda steps to the front door.

There was a pause in her stride as she entered the foyer, pushing the door shut behind her and turning to the study that had orginally been the front parlor of the old house. The solid oak doors slid open at the touch of her hand, bringing the conversation within to an abrupt end.

Her heart was squeezed by the harrowed and worried lines that aged her father's face twenty years. The instant his gaze lighted on her face, his expression underwent a transformation—the tension smoothing into a welcoming smile of false unconcern. This sudden attempt to mask his feelings puzzled and frightened Glenna. What was he trying to hide?

Walking toward his chair, Glenna fixed a smile on her mouth while her eyes searched his face. But her poker-playing father revealed none of his inner thoughts. If she had knocked at the study door she wouldn't have seen even that brief glimpse of his inner anxiety.

"Had you started to wonder where I was?" Her voice was cheerful as she deposited her camera and notebook on the sturdy oak desk before she reached his chair. Resting a hand on the chair arm, Glenna bent down to brush her lips to the pallor of his cheeks, a color that had become natural to his complexion.

"I hadn't," Orin Reynolds insisted with a bright sparkle in his eyes. "I knew you would wander in sooner or later, but I think Bruce was becoming concerned whether you were going to show up."

Glenna straightened and looked in the direction her father had glanced. Bruce Hawkins was standing beside the fireplace, a shoulder leaning against the marble mantlepiece. His blue gaze was warmly admiring in its inspection of her, taking in the wind-tossed curls of her chestnut hair, the loose-fitting velour sweater the color of butter cream draping the swelling mounds of her breasts, and the slimness of her hips and long legs in her brushed-denim jeans. The frank appreciation in his look held a hint of reserve, out of respect for her father's presence.

"Where have you been?" Bruce asked the question her father hadn't. There was nothing interrogating in it, just casual interest.

"Communing with Mother Nature," Glenna replied.

Her gray green eyes swept his straw-colored hair and square-jawed face. Bruce was good-looking, intelligent, and ambitious. Since her father's first attack more than two years ago, he had assumed more and more responsibility for the operation of the Reynoldses' coal mine.

It was really only after her father's first heart attack that Glenna had become acquainted with him. The relationship between them had grown slowly until it had reached its present point where they were more than friends but not quite lovers.

Glenna was fully aware that she was the one unwilling to let their relationship progress any further. Her hesitancy was something that confused Glenna. Bruce appeared to represent all that she desired in a man, yet some vital ingredient seemed to be missing. Its lack kept her from making any firm commitment.

Sometimes she thought it was a loyalty to her father that made her hold back. Other times, like now, Glenna simply didn't know why she was reluctant. One word from her, one indication of acceptance, and she knew Bruce would propose.

"Communing with nature," Bruce repeated her answer. "With your eye on the plan to write a series of articles, I'll wager."

"You guessed right," Glenna agreed, leaving the uncertainty of her feelings toward Bruce to be examined at a later time. "That's one thing about free-lancing; I can slant an article so many different ways that I can sell the same story line to several different periodicals."

"And your head is buzzing with all of the ideas," her father surmised.

The softness of her throaty laugh was an affirmative answer, because it had been true when she entered the study although a whole new set of thoughts had subsequently supplanted the ideas for the nature-oriented articles.

"There's some coffee in the pot yet. Would you like a cup?" Bruce offered, moving to the china coffee service sitting on the oblong coffee table in front of the sofa.

Briefly, Glenna resented this extension of hospitality in her own home, but she quelled it. Bruce's familiarity was something both she and her father had invited. Besides, there was a certain thoughtfulness in his request. She wondered at her sudden sensitivity to the situation.

"I'd love some, thank you." She took a seat on the sofa while he poured a cup and handed it to her. Black, with no sugar, the way she liked it. Bruce sank his lean frame onto the cushion beside her, an arm automatically seeking the backrest of the sofa behind her head, but he didn't touch her.

"How are things at the mine?" The question from Glenna was an absent one, issued automatically, a polite inquiry because it was Bruce's province.

Glenna glanced over the rim of her coffee cup in time to see Bruce dart a sharp look at her father. Then he replied, too blandly, "Fine."

Instantly she knew there was a problem. A serious one. She sipped at her coffee, using the action to hide her knowledge while her mind raced back to the anxious expression on her father's face when she had entered the room.

"I invited Bruce to dinner this evening," her father informed her with a subtle change of subject. "Hannah assured me the main dish would stretch to feed four. The way she cooks I can never decide whether she is trying to fatten us up or trying to feed an army. The woman always cooks enough for ten people."

"Heaven knows you need some fattening up," Glenna observed, commenting on his weight loss that had made his usually brawny frame appear gaunt. But she knew he disliked any discussion of his health and turned to Bruce. "You are staying?" The lilt of her voice changed the statement into a question.

"I never turn down an invitation for a home-cooked meal or the company of a lovely young woman." His casually worded answer was at war with the flattering intensity of his look.

Glenna teased him deliberately. "I shall have to warn Hannah that you have designs on her, as well as her cooking."

Bruce chuckled, amused by her response. The movement of her father's hand distracted her attention. He was reaching automatically into the breast pocket of his shirt for a cigarette. Orin Reynolds had quit smoking after his first heart attack. Only in moments of severe stress did the habit reassert itself. His shirt pocket no longer held a pack of cigarettes. Glenna noticed the faint tremor of his hand when it was lowered to the armrest. It was not a withdrawal symptom from smoking.

"After two years, you can't still want a

cigarette, dad," she chided to make him aware she had seen his action. It didn't prompt the reaction she wanted.

Just for a second the facade of well-being slipped to reveal an expression that appeared supremely tired and defeated. A chill raced down Glenna's spine at the sullenness in his gray eyes before he laughed gruffly. Something was very wrong. Glenna only wished that she knew what it was.

"After two years I am craving the taste of tobacco. There are times when heaven to me is a smoke-filled poker room with whiskey and cigarettes amid a raucous backdrop of fiddle music instead of fluffy clouds, halos, and harps," he joked. "There are times when the quality of life outweighs the quantity."

"That is a rather morbid observation, dad," Glenna forced a smile, but she was aware that there was very little color in her cheeks. She saw the grain of truth in his words, but her father had always been a fighter, battling the odds stacked against him. His remark had smacked of surrender. It wasn't something she could understand, even issued in jest.

"I suppose it is, but sometimes I. . . ." He stopped and breathed out a sigh. His mouth twitched into a rueful smile, vitality dancing back to glitter in his eyes. "I guess I'm tired."

"Why don't you lie down for a few minutes before dinner?" Glenna suggested. "I'll keep Bruce company."

"Did you hear that, Bruce?" her father

mocked. "She sounds so concerned about me, doesn't she? But a father knows when his daughter doesn't want him around."

Her fingers tightened on the curved handle of her coffee cup. It was action designed to keep Glenna from leaping to her feet to help her father out of the chair. He hated any acknowledgment of the weakness of his muscles. It was a slow process, but he rose, unaided, to walk stiffly from the room.

Her throat was hurting by the time she heard the study door slide shut behind him. She stared at the coffee in the china cup she was holding so tightly. There was a stony clarity to her eyes— eyes that had become strangers to tears.

"What is wrong at the mine, Bruce?" she demanded without looking up.

A second of pregnant silence was followed by a hollow laugh. "I don't know what you are talking about. Nothing is wrong at the mine."

"It must be very serious for both you and dad to lie to me." Glenna set the cup on the table with a briskness that rattled it against its saucer.

She rose so abruptly that she dislodged the sunglasses from their perch atop her head. Impatiently she removed them and folded the bows with a decisive snap before setting them on the table, too.

Heavily fringed with lashes, her eyes narrowed their gaze on Bruce. "I want to know what it is."

"There isn't anything you can do." He looked grim.

"You don't know that," she retorted. "I haven't heard any talk of a wildcat strike. And I can't believe the miners would walk out on dad like that, anyway. If it's a labor problem, surely dad can iron it out if you can't."

"It isn't labor." He avoided her gaze, his jaw hardening.

Glenna frowned. With that possibility eliminated, she was at a loss to guess the cause. "Then what is it? You are a mining engineer so it can't be anything technical."

"It's the government." The hint that his skill was being questioned forced Bruce into supplying the reason.

"What? Taxes?" She couldn't imagine her father getting into a position where he was delinquent in employee taxes.

"Nothing so simple," Bruce replied in a scoffing breath and pushed to his feet. He shoved his hands into the hip pockets of his slacks, an action that pushed his shoulders back and stretched the material of his blue shirt across the sinewed width of his chest. "The mine failed its safety inspection."

"How bad is it?" Glenna heard the dullness in her voice, the feeling of dread sweeping over her.

"They are issuing an injunction to shut the mine down within thirty days if the necessary steps aren't taken immediately to correct the situation," he announced in a voice as leaden as her own.

"Surely you can appeal the ruling—gain more time," she argued.

"That's what I've been doing for the last year and a half," he snapped in a sudden blaze of temper. "We ran out of time. There won't be any more postponements."

Parallel furrows ran across her forehead. "If you knew it was coming, why didn't you take steps to correct the problem?" Glenna challenged in a spate of responding anger. "Why did you leave it until the last minute? I suppose you just dumped this all on dad this afternoon—when it's practically too late to do anything to stop it. No wonder he acted so defeated. He isn't well. He trusted you to—"

"Orin has known from the start!" Bruce interrupted sharply. "If I'd had my choice, I would have begun implementing and installing new safety measures. But I didn't have any say in the matter."

"Are you implying that my father knowingly endangered the lives of the miners?" The accusation brought a pronounced silver glitter to her eyes, making them icy and more gray than green.

"For God's sake! He had no more choice in the matter than I did."

He turned away to rest an arm on the mantle of the fireplace, bending his head to rub his hand over his mouth and chin in a gesture of exasperation and futility.

Her anger dissipated at his attitude of helplessness. "What do you mean? Why didn't he have a choice?" Glenna frowned. "You said yourself that the solution was to comply."

"That costs money, Glenna," Bruce sighed and straightened to look at her. "That's why the initial ruling was appealed to gain time to raise the capital to make the changes and install the necessary devices."

"He could borrow it. The bank would loan him the—"

"No. Orin took out second and third mortgates on everything he owned to pull the mine through the strike we had two and a half years ago. Once he could have borrowed on his reputation alone, but after these last two heart attacks he's had—" Bruce filled the pause with an expressive shrug of his shoulders "—the lending institutions regard him as an uninsurable risk with overextended credit."

Dark clouds of despair began to enfold her in their arms. Glenna felt chilled and struggled to elude their murky envelopment. Her gaze clung to Bruce's handsome features.

"Surely there has to be someone who will help dad." She tried to sound calm, and not nearly as desperate as she felt.

In her mind the thoughts kept turning over and over. If the mine was closed it would ultimately mean bankruptcy. They would lose the house and everything of any value. The effect such a situation would have on her father was something Glenna didn't want to contemplate. She barely succeeded in suppressing a shudder.

"On your father's instructions, I sent out feelers to see if Coulson Mining would be interested in a merger with your father's company—on the

chance they might see some tax advantages."
Bruce shook his head grimly. "Their reply was a
flat 'not interested.'"

"Coulson Mining," Glenna repeated. "Jett
Coulson's company? The coal magnate."

"Coal, gas, you name it and he's rolling in
it—including gold," Bruce nodded.

With startling clarity Glenna recalled the
mental picture of a grainy newspaper photograph she had seen of Jett Coulson when she
had been reading a trade journal to her father
shortly after his first heart attack. The man's
hair and eyes had appeared as black as the shining coal that had built his fortune. At the time
of the photograph he had been in his mid-
thirties, yet his features had been lined with a
toughness beyond his years.

To Glenna, Jett Coulson had seemed all
rough, raw manhood. Yet her father had spok-
en of him with respect, she remembered. What
she had viewed as ruthlessness in his features,
her father had regarded as strength. Jett
Coulson's lack of polish and refinement made
him a man the miners could understand and
believe, even when they disagreed. It was said
that Jett Coulson never lied. The standing joke
was that a lot of people wished he would.

"Did you talk to Jett Coulson?" she asked,
clinging to the one tantalizing straw Bruce had
offered.

"Are you kidding?" he laughed harshly.
"I'm nothing but a manager—a mining engineer. I talked to one of his underlings."

"There wasn't even a crumb of interest," Glenna persisted.

"Be realistic, Glenna," Bruce sighed. "Why should Coulson agree to a merger when he'll probably be able to pick the mine up for nothing in a few months. Why should he bail your father out of this mess? He's never had a reputation for being a good samaritan. It's unlikely he'll have a change of heart at this late date."

"No, I suppose not." Her shoulders slumped in defeat. She turned away to walk to a front window to gaze sightlessly at the shadows gathering on the lawn. "What's going to happen to daddy?" She wasn't aware she had murmured the aching question aloud.

Approaching her from behind, Bruce rubbed his hands over her arms. "Glenna, I'm sorry. I wish there was some way I could help...something I could do to prevent this."

She heard the echo of futility in his voice, the forlorn emptiness of his offer. When his arms curved around her and his jaw rested against her hair, there was no comfort in his embrace.

"I haven't got much money, but when the mine closes—" he began.

"*If* the mine closes, not *when*, Bruce," Glenna quickly corrected him and moved out of his arms and away from the window. Her back was ramrod straight when she turned to regard him. "It will be thirty days, you said, until the injunction takes effect. A lot can happen in thirty days."

"You sound like your father." He eyed her sadly. "Don't be a fool, Glenna."

His remarks only served to make her more determined. If her father hadn't given up hope yet, neither would she. Her patrician features took on an air of resolve. The sunlight glinting through the window set the deep auburn hue of her brown hair afire, as if reinforcing her purpose.

"A Reynolds doesn't give up without putting up one helluva fight first. Dad isn't the type to lie down and let the world step on him. And neither am I."

"I don't think you understand what you are up against." Bruce shook his head, but didn't attempt to argue too strongly. "There is a time for pride...and a time to be sensible. I should know, Glenna. I've fought this day for a year and a half. You can think what you like about me, but after a year and a half of butting my head against a stone wall, I know when to quit."

"Is that what you are going to do? Quit?" Her lip curled in a contemptuous challenge.

"Not literally. No, I'll see this thing through to the bitter end." There was absolutely no doubt in his expression about what the end would be. Turning, he walked to the desk and picked up the briefcase lying atop it. "I think it would be better if I took a rain check on the dinner invitation tonight. I don't think either of us would be very good company. Make my apologies to Orin, will you?" he murmured quietly.

"Of course." Glenna accepted his decision

with a curt nod and made no attempt to walk with him to the front door.

His glance was faintly mocking when he crossed the room and paused at the sliding oak doors. "I'll show myself out," he said, taunting her lack of courtesy.

"I know you will," she replied coolly.

CHAPTER TWO

THE TINGLING SHOWER SPRAY drummed out some of her tension. The raking wire claws of the hairbrush eliminated more of it while untangling her wind-snarled hair. Makeup and a floral, silk shirtwaist bolstered her spirits.

When she met her father in the dining room she felt capable of taking on any obstacle—including the stone wall Bruce had referred to. Which was just as well because she was subjected to her father's sharp-eyed scrutiny the minute she entered the room.

"Hannah tells me Bruce decided not to stay for dinner. Did you two have a lover's quarrel?" He sat in his accustomed chair at the head of the claw-footed dining-room table.

"We aren't lovers so that isn't possible." She pulled out the chair on his right and sat down. She denied his allegation with ease, not at all upset by the presumption he had made concerning her relationship with Bruce.

An iron-gray eyebrow was raised. "You obviously had a difference of opinion about something."

"We did." Glenna agreed with a quick smile

as she spread the Irish-linen napkin across her lap. "It was over the closing of the mine. He regarded it as inevitable. I didn't." She saw the look of consternation spread across his face and turned her attention to the housekeeper entering the room with a tureen of soup. "Hmm, that smells good, Hannah." She sniffed the air appreciatively, the warm aroma of chicken stock wafting from the china serving bowl.

"Homemade. I spent all afternoon fixing the noodles," the plump woman retorted with her usual sassy spirit. "And you'd better do more than pick at my food tonight, Orin Reynolds, or else I'll stick you in a high chair and spoon-feed you. If you think I can't do it, you just try me," she threatened and set the tureen on the table near Glenna with a decisive thump.

Her father barely noticed the housekeeper, who had practically become an adopted member of the family. Aware that his silence was generated by her reference to the trouble at the mine, Glenna took over the task of ladling the homemade chicken soup into the individual bowls.

"Dad loves your homemade egg noodles, Hannah," Glenna assured the woman sternly eyeing Orin Reynold's bowed head. "Don't you?" she prompted and set a bowl of the steaming soup in front of him.

"How did you find out about the mine?" He lifted his gaze to her face. His expression was a little stunned, a little disbelieving and tinted with relief.

"Did you really think you could keep it from me?" she chided and dished a bowl of soup for herself. "I simply asked Bruce outright what the problem was at the mine. I saw how worried you looked when I first came in. Bruce isn't as good a poker player as you are. It was a simple deduction that whatever was bothering you, it had to do with the mine. After that it was a simple matter of putting a few pointed questions to Bruce." She shrugged her shoulders in an indication of how easy it had been to get the answers from him.

The curving line of his mouth held faint bemusement. "I doubt if it was hard to get the answers from him. You have Hawkins wrapped around your little finger. He'd do or say anything to please you, you know that, don't you?"

It wasn't really a question so much as it was an observation. Glenna flicked him a dry glance, reading between the lines of his comment.

"Don't decide to try any matchmaking, dad." She filled the last soup bowl and leaned across the table to set it where Hannah would be sitting. "I'll choose my own future husband, thank you." Moving the soup tureen to the center of the table, Glenna returned the conversation to its original topic, the coal mine and its problems. "Why didn't you tell me about the trouble you were having?"

"I didn't want to cause you any needless worry." He picked up his soupspoon and dipped it into the bowl, but made no attempt to lift a spoonful to his mouth. "I never thought it would come to this point," her father admitted as Hannah returned to the dining room with a basket of homemade saltine crackers to go with the soup. "I was positive that between us, Bruce and I would come up with a solution that would keep the mine from being shut down. I wasn't really trying to keep it from you. I just didn't want you worrying over something you couldn't do anything about. You have enough on your mind."

"What's this about the mine being shut down?" Hannah demanded. A frown of concern narrowed her eyes. "When did all this come about? And eat your soup. Stop playing with it," she ordered without a pause.

"The mine doesn't meet the safety standards. Unless it complies, the government is shutting it down," Glenna explained quickly and a little absently since it was old news to her. She barely noticed the faint shock that spread across Hannah's face as the plump woman sank into the chair opposite her. Challenge glinted in the look Glenna cast at her father. "So what are you going to do? Quit? That seems to be the opinion Bruce has."

"We have exhausted just about every avenue of hope," Orin sighed. Leaving the spoon in the bowl, he rested his elbows on the table and clasped his hands together to form an upright triangle with the table top, pressing his fingers to his mouth. There was grim resignation in his features. "I'm at a complete loss to know which way to turn."

The housekeeper glared at him. "Orin Reynolds, I have never known you to give up."

He lifted his head, sending the frazzle-haired woman an irritated look. "Who said I was? I just don't know where to go from here."

Glenna smiled at the fighting spirit displayed by that response. It was reassuring, and reinforced her own determination. To her father the future wasn't as dark and foreboding as Bruce regarded it.

"Bruce indicated that was the way you felt," she said. "So do I."

They exchanged glances. The underlying strain that had tautened his features faded at her supportive remark. His expression became touched with a reminiscent warmth and affection.

"There are times when you remind me so much of your mother. God bless her soul," he murmured. "She always stood beside me no matter what." After a touching pause he added, "I miss her."

The sighing comment was a needless admission. The love her parents shared had been one of the greatest securities of Glenna's childhood. She was aware how keenly her father had felt the loss of his wife to cancer three years ago. It had been mercifully swift, but Glenna suspected that her mother's death had precipitated his heart attack a short year later. For a while she had feared he had a subconscious death wish to join his beloved Mary, but his will to live was strong.

"What on earth are you going to do?" the housekeeper questioned, then grimaced. "The soup is getting cold. If you had terrible news like this, why did you wait until I had food on the table before bringing it up? It would have been so much easier, Orin, if you had talked about this before dinner...or afterward, but not in the middle of a meal." She sent him a disgruntled look. "You haven't answered my question. What are you going to do?" Hannah ignored the fact that she hadn't given him an opportunity to reply.

"I don't know." He shook his head and reached for the spoon resting in his soup bowl. "We seem to be up against a brick wall."

"If you can't knock it down, there has to be a way to go around it, under it, or over it," Glenna reasoned.

"I thought we had a way around it," he agreed with her logic, his mouth twisting ruefully. "Unfortunately it turned out to be a dead end."

"You are referring to merging with Coulson Mining?" she guessed.

The spoon he held was poised in midair, halfway to his mouth, the broth dripping off the edge into the bowl as Orin shot her a quick look. "You know about that, too?" he said with faint surprise. "It doesn't sound like Bruce left anything out."

"Not much," she admitted.

He carried the spoon the rest of the way to his mouth and swallowed the soup broth it contained. Returning the spoon to the bowl, he reached for one of Hannah's crackers and began buttering.it, as if he needed something to do with his hands.

"Did Bruce also tell you that he suggested a meeting with the miners to let them know about the situation and the possibility the mine will be closed in a month?" His gaze slid from the cracker to Glenna.

She attacked her soup, angered again by Bruce's defeatist attitude. "I certainly hope you put him straight on that score," she stated in a vigorous rejection of the plan.

"I agreed with him." Her father didn't meet her stunned look as he took abnormal interest in evenly spreading the butter over his cracker. "He's setting the meeting between shift changes tomorrow afternoon."

The announcement shocked Glenna. It seemed to indicate a surrender to the inevitable, which was a direct contradiction to all of his previous statements. She returned the soup-spoon to its place beside the rest of the silver-ware, mindless of the broth stain it made on the tablecloth.

"You aren't serious," she protested incredulously.

"It is the only fair thing to do, Glenna." His voice was patiently reasoning. "If—" He paused to reemphasize the qualifying word. "If the mine is going to be closed, the miners should know about it before it happens so they have a chance to prepare for the layoff."

"But you are going to try to find a way to keep it operating, so why tell them?" She didn't understand.

"I feel we should prepare them for the worst that could happen." It was an unequivocal statement of his belief. Put that way, it didn't sound quite so bad. A heavy sigh brought an air of sadness to her father. "It wouldn't be so tragic if I was the only one who would suffer from the closing of the mine, but so many people's lives are involved. The economy of this whole community revolves around the Reynolds Mine. We'll have our own minature depression in this valley."

"It isn't as if you aren't trying to do something to prevent it." Glenna refused to let him blame himself for any repercussions that might occur.

"I know." He smiled at her encouragement. "I'm fighting just as hard for myself as I am for them. After all, I stand to lose everything including this house where Mary and I spent so many wonderful years—" The tightness in his throat cut the sentence short as his gaze made a sweep of the room. It ended its arc to linger on the housekeeper. "Even you would be affected by the closing of the mine, dear Hannah." He reached out to cover the housekeeper's hand with his own, a gesture that revealed the affection he felt toward the irascible woman. "You would be out of a job and a place to live. I had always intended for you to have a tidy pension to retire on, but I doubt if I could afford to give you severance pay."

"Don't you go trying to force your charity on me, Orin Reynolds." Hannah pulled her hand from beneath his, rejecting his apology, but the gruffness of her voice revealed how deeply moved she was by his remarks. "I can look out for myself. I always have, haven't I?"

"Of course," he smiled benignly.

"The mine isn't shut down, and we haven't been turned out of this house yet." Glenna felt the need to point that out. "So let's concentrate our attention on trying to prevent it, instead of deciding what we will do if it happens."

"Any suggestions?" It wasn't a taunting request from her father, merely an acknowledgment that he could think of no more avenues to explore.

"Aren't there other mining companies that might be interested in a merger besides Coulson? Just because Coulson isn't interested doesn't mean another company might not be," she reasoned.

"Considering the mine's indebtedness and the investment capital needed to bring it up to standard, only a large corporation could absorb us—a company that could take advantage of the tax benefits. The only company that fits that bill is Jett Coulson's. And you know what his answer was," he murmured dryly.

"It wasn't his answer," Glenna remembered.

"It came from one of his underlings. Bruce said so."

"But I'm sure it came down from him."

"You don't know that."

Her father studied her for a minute, silently following her train of thought. "You think I should get the answer straight from the horse's mouth, so to speak."

"Why not?" she shrugged. "You haven't personally spoken to him. Neither has Bruce. As competent as Bruce might be as a manager, that doesn't mean he's equally as competent to present your merger proposition." She watched him mulling over her comment.

"You could be right," he conceded thoughtfully. "Maybe I should arrange a meeting with Jett Coulson."

"Absolutely," Glenna nodded as she watched the hope being reborn in his gray eyes. "What have you got to lose?"

"Absolutely nothing." He spooned some homemade soup into his mouth and tasted its flavor for the first time. His bright gaze darted to the housekeeper, a smile of approval curving his mouth. "This is delicious, Hannah."

"Of course it is," the housekeeper sniffed, as if there could be any doubt she would serve less than the best.

LATE THE FOLLOWING AFTERNOON, Glenna was in her bedroom. One corner of the room was a miniature study, a small desk cubbyholed amid the bookshelves. A portable typewriter sat in the center of the orderly chaos, a sheet of paper in its carriage, and her notes from the previous day's outing scattered around the desk top.

A knock at the door intruded on Glenna's frowning concentration, turning her head from the scribbled handwriting she was trying to decipher. Before she could respond to the summoning knock, the door opened to admit her father.

"We're in luck," he announced, entering the room with more buoyancy to his stride than she had seen in a long time.

She pushed all thoughts of the article she was trying to write from her mind and directed all her attention to him. A faint smile touched her mouth as she studied his jovial mood.

"What kind of luck are we in?" Glenna joked and tucked the thickness of her auburn hair behind an ear. "Good or bad?"

"Anything would have to be an improvement over what we've had so it must be good." Despite his surface vigor, he sought out the plump armchair covered in toasted-gold corduroy. It was an indication of how fleeting his strength was, his lack of stamina.

Glenna was careful to ignore it. "Are you going to tell me what this good luck is, or keep me in suspense?"

"I just found out in a roundabout way that Jett Coulson is going to be entertaining some of his lobbyists at Greenbrier this weekend." His smile fairly beamed from his face.

His announcement merely drew a frown from

Glenna. "And that is the good luck?" She failed to see what was so wonderful about it.

"It certainly is. Meeting him there will allow a casual approach," he explained. "If I made an appointment to see Coulson at his office there would undoubtedly be a hundred and one interruptions, and his time would be limited. At the inn, I'll have more than one chance to discuss it with him."

It sounded very logical but Glenna saw a problem. "But if he's entertaining, won't he—"

"It's only an excuse to party. Coulson will have plenty of free time," her father assured.

"Are you sure this is the course you should take?" She wasn't convinced. "Wouldn't it be wiser to meet him in an atmosphere more conducive to business?"

Her father chuckled. "More business deals are consummated at social gatherings than are ever accomplished in a corporate office. Once an agreement is reached, it's up·to the attorneys to work out the fine details. A handshake from Coulson over the dinner table is as good as cash in the bank."

"You certainly know more about such things than I do," Glenna conceded and shifted in her chair to hook a leg beneath her.

"How long do you think it will take to drive from here to White Sulphur Springs? I'd like to arrive around noon on Friday."

"It shouldn't take more than two or three hours," she guessed.

"You will be my chauffeur, won't you?" her

father asked, well aware that his doctor would be against him driving that distance alone.

"I'm certainly not going to let you go by yourself." Then she hesitated. "Are you sure you wouldn't rather have Bruce with you?"

"That would be much too obvious." He shook his head, rejecting her suggestion. "I want it to appear to be a father-daughter outing, all very casual. A weekend vacation will be good for you anyway. Besides, you can pick up a lot of material for your writing."

"I'm sure I could, but—" Glenna paused uncertainly, eyeing her father with concern. "Dad, do you think we can afford this?"

"At this point a few hundred dollars isn't going to keep us out of bankruptcy court." His expression became serious. "This is the last roll of the dice. We might as well shoot our whole wad and go out in style."

"You have always been a first-class gambler, dad." She observed with a faint smile that held warmth but no humor.

"Be sure to pack our best clothes." Her father stood up, the decision made and irrevocable now. "We don't want to look like a pair of beggars when we meet Coulson."

THE WHITE MAGNIFICENCE of the Greenbrier was nestled in an upland Allegheny valley. Its forested lawns and mountain backdrop provided the beauty of natural surroundings. The famed spa and its predecessor, Old White, obtained its initial notoriety from the soothing mineral waters that smelled like an egg that was half boiled and half spoiled. Yet its guest register over the years included an impressive list of celebrities.

This was not Glenna's first visit to the famous West Virginia resort, but she was still awed by its stately elegance and aura of steeped tradition. The many-storied facade was pristine white with a columned portico entrance worthy of the grandest and noblest of guests.

After they had registered and been shown to their adjoining rooms, she and her father had split up. Glenna had wanted to do some exploring and familiarize herself again with the hotel complex while her father wanted to make inquiries and learn the most logical place to "bump into" Jett Coulson.

Her wandering walk brought Glenna into the facility housing the indoor tennis courts. She paused to watch a match being played on the near court, two couples playing a game of mixed doubles. The good-natured ribbing that was exchanged back and forth between the pairs brought a smile to her face.

A shouted reference to the time directed her glance at her watch. It was a few minutes past three o'clock. By the time she returned to her room and changed into her swimsuit, she would have an hour to swim before meeting her father. The fairness of her skin, the complexion of a true redhead, forced Glenna to avoid the sun during the middle of the day when its burning rays did the most damage.

As she started to move away from the near

tennis court, a hoot of laughter attracted her attention. Turning her head, she glanced over her shoulder. In the split second when she wasn't watching where she was going, she nearly walked into another player. Her forward progress was halted by a pair of hands that stopped her before she ran into him.

Her attention was jerked to the front; a hurried apology forming on her lips. It froze there for a full second as Glenna stared at the tall sun-bronzed figure of a man in white tennis shorts and white knit top. A black pair of eyes were returning her stunned regard with a shimmer of bemusement as he removed his hands from her shoulders.

Glenna was struck by the irony of the situation. She had accidentally run into the man that her father was contriving to bump into. A smile played with the corners of her mouth, attracting his interest.

"I'm sorry, Mr. Coulson," she apologized smoothly. "I'm afraid I wasn't paying attention to where I was going."

An eyebrow flicked upward at the use of his name. All the toughness was there in his features, just as she had remembered from the photograph she had seen. But the photograph hadn't captured the perpetual gleam in his dark eyes—the gleam of a rogue wolf.

"Have we met before?" Like his gaze, his voice had a certain directness to it. Glenna was subjected to the boldness of his sweeping glance. "I can't believe I would have forgotten meeting you."

The line was delivered smoothly, so smoothly that Glenna found it hard to question its sincerity. "We've never been introduced. I recognized you from a newspaper photograph," she explained and felt warmed by the slow smile that spread across his mouth.

"You must have a very good memory. It's been some time since there have been any articles about me, Miss—" He paused deliberately to invite Glenna to fill in the blank.

"Reynolds. Glenna Reynolds." She found herself becoming intrigued by this man that she had once labeled as ruthless. There was a reckless gambler's charm about him that she hadn't expected. This, plus the unwavering determination etched in his craggy features, made a potent combination. She began to feel the force of it exerting its influence on her. She hadn't anticipated being sexually disturbed by Jett Coulson.

"That name sounds familiar to me. Glenna Reynolds." He repeated it as if to jog his memory, his eyes narrowing faintly.

"Perhaps you have—" She started to explain who her father was, but Jett Coulson interrupted her with a snap of his fingers in recollection.

"Glenna Renolds was the by-line on an article that was in the magazine section of the Sunday paper. Was that yours?" His look became thoughtful, a degree of aloofness entering his expression.

"Yes, it was," Glenna admitted with faint astonishment. "I'm flattered that you read it... and remembered it."

"I remembered it because of the way you managed to take a boring subject and made it appear interesting," he replied diffidently.

"Thank you... I think." She qualified her statement because she wasn't sure that his remark hadn't been a backhanded compliment. It irritated Glenna to think he might be mocking her behind his poker-smooth exterior.

"Is this a business trip or pleasure?" His observing gaze seemed to take note of the turbulence clouding her gray green eyes, yet he had shifted the subject so smoothly that Glenna wondered if she hadn't imagined the gibe in the last.

"Both," she admitted.

"The Greenbrier has been written about many times."

"Then my challenge will be to do it differently." There was a defensive tilt to her chin, elevating it a degree. She became conscious of his superior height and his unshakable self-assurance.

"I enjoy a challenge myself," he murmured. Then he inclined his head in a slight nod. "Excuse me, but I have a tennis date to keep."

His comment prompted Glenna to move to one side as if she had been blocking him, which she hadn't. His tanned and sinewed legs carried him past her with long strides. Her gaze followed him for several seconds, taking note of the narrowness of his waist and hips tapering out to the breadth of his ropy shoulders. There was little doubt in her mind that Jett Coulson was a breed of man she had never encountered before—and was unlikely to meet again. He was one of a kind.

CHAPTER THREE

ORIN REYNOLDS was at the poolside when Glenna climbed the ladder out of the swimming pool. She sensed an air of urgency about him as she walked, leaving a trail of water behind her, to the deck chair where she'd left her towel and flowered robe.

"Hi!" When she greeted him, she was slightly out of breath from the swim, but exhilarated by the activity. Within seconds after leaving the pool, the evaporation of water cooled her skin and began raising goosebumps. Glenna shook out the towel and began briskly rubbing herself down. "What's up? I thought we were going to meet in the room."

"I tipped the bellboy. He told me that Coulson usually has a cocktail in the lounge before dinner. I wanted to be sure we got there before he did so we could spot him coming in."

Unsnapping her bathing cap, she took it off to let her auburn hair tumble free. "I bumped into him—literally—at the tennis court this afternoon."

"Coulson?" Her father appeared to need reassurance that they were talking about the same person.

"The one and only." She used the towel to blot the excess moisture from her swimsuit, a sleek one-piece suit of sea green.

"What did he say?" Her father was keenly alert, studying every nuance of her expression. "Does he know who you are?"

"He doesn't know that I'm your daughter—at least I didn't tell him I was. But he had read one of my articles and remembered my name from that." Which was something she was still a little surprised about. "That was just about the extent of our conversation."

"Mmm." Orin Reynolds seemed to digest that information while Glenna slipped into the loose-fitting floral robe and hooked the wide belt around her slim waistline. "Do you have shoes?"

"Under the chair." She knelt to remove the fashionably heeled slip-ons from beneath the chair. Using his arm for balance, she stepped into first one, then the other.

"Let's go to the lounge." He took her arm and started to lead her away.

Glenna stopped in stunned protest. "I can't go to the lounge like this."

"Nonsense. It's informal. There will be people there in tennis shorts. You are certainly more fully clothed than that." He dismissed her protest.

Glenna didn't attempt to argue about her wearing apparel. "But I haven't any lipstick—any makeup on." Her fingers touched the damp tendrils of curling hair. "And my hair—"

"Nothing you could do would improve on perfection." Deliberately he was too lavish in his praise, mocking her vanity.

"Dad, be serious," she sighed, unable to stay upset by his high-handedness.

"If you are determined to spoil that fresh clean look, use the powder room to comb your hair and put on some lipstick," he conceded with an indulging smile. "But don't take long. I don't want to miss him."

After Glenna had made the necessary repairs to her appearance she met her father at the entrance to the lounge. It was just beginning to fill with the happy-hour crowd. Orin Reynolds guided her to a table strategically located to permit him to observe the door. Their drink order was served—a glass of white wine for Glenna and a Perrier with a lime twist for her father. She had taken her first sip of the wine when Jett Coulson entered the lounge alone. She touched her father's arm to draw attention to the man inside the doorway, but it was unnecessary. Orin had already spotted him.

Those gleaming dark eyes were making a slow inspection of the room, not in search of anyone as far as Glenna could tell, but simply taking note of who was present. Her father stood up, attracting Jett's attention. His gaze narrowed as it touched Glenna, then returned to her father.

"Mr. Coulson." Without raising his voice from its pleasant pitch, her father succeeded in summoning Jett to their table. "I haven't had the pleasure of meeting you formally. My name is Orin Reynolds, of the Reynolds Mine.''

There was a firm clasping of hands as Jett murmured a polite, "How do you do, Mr. Reynolds.''

If her father's name or that of his coal mine, meant anything to Jett, Glenna didn't see any recognition register in his expression. But she was coming to mistrust those hardened features to reveal his inner thoughts.

"I believe you met my daughter Glenna earlier this afternoon," her father said, by way of acknowledging her presence.

"Yes, we...bumped into each other." The faint pause carried an inflection of dry amusement as Jett nodded to her. "Hello, again, Miss Reynolds.''

"Hello, Mr. Coulson." There was a husky pitch to her voice, and Glenna wasn't sure exactly where it had come from. She seemed to be holding her breath, too, without knowing why.

No longer dressed in his tennis clothes, he had changed into a pair of navy slacks and a silk shirt in a subdued blue design against a cream background. The untamed thickness of his hair held a sheen of dampness, prompting Glenna to surmise he had probably showered. She had been so fully prepared to dislike him; now she found herself wondering why she didn't.

"Sit down," her father invited. "Let me buy you a drink." Then he paused, as if suddenly realizing. "Were you meeting someone?"

"No." He chose to sit in the empty chair beside Glenna, across the table from her father.

"What will you have to drink?" Orin signaled to the cocktail waitress.

"Scotch, neat, on the rocks," Jett ordered and her father passed the information on.

"Who won your tennis match?" Seated this close, Glenna inhaled the tangy scent of his after-shave with each breath she took. It stimulated her senses, awakening them to his rough brand of masculinity.

"I did." The reply was neither a boast nor a brag, merely a simple statement of fact.

"Naturally," she murmured dryly, goaded by the sheer confidence of his statement.

He turned his head to regard her with those gleaming, but impassive black eyes. "I always play to win."

"Don't you ever play simply for the fun of competing?" Even as she asked the question she remembered her first conclusion that he could be ruthless.

"That's the rationale of a loser." A half-smile tugged at the corners of his mouth, taunting her. Then he let his gaze slide back to her father. "I would never have guessed she was your daughter, Mr. Reynolds."

"Please, call me Orin," her father insisted and cast a smiling glance at her. "No, there isn't much of a resemblance between us. Thankfully, Glenna takes after her mother, God rest her soul. She was a strikingly beautiful woman, like Glenna."

"Don't mind him. He's prejudiced." For the first time she was embarrassed by her father's compliments. Usually when he made such remarks about her looks in front of friends or strangers, she just smiled and let them pass by without comment. This time they made her uncomfortable. Or was it the dark and knowing regard of the man sitting beside her?

Jett's Scotch was served. The interruption allowed conversation to drift to another topic, much to Glenna's relief.

"Tell me, Orin, what brings you here?" Jett questioned with mild interest. "Your daughter mentioned that she was here on a combination of business and pleasure. Is that true for you, too?"

Glenna hastened to explain. "I told Mr. Coulson of my intention to write a travel article about Greenbrier."

"Glenna has quite a talent with words. I believe she said you had read some of her work," her father attempted to dodge the initial question.

"Yes, I have," Jett admitted but didn't repeat the comment he'd made to Glenna when they'd met before. "Do you help with the research?"

"No," Orin denied with a throaty laugh. "She does everything herself. I don't know which of us is chaperoning the other. I can't say that this is strictly a pleasure trip for me since a businessman never escapes his responsibilities, not even for a weekend. I'm sure you know what I mean."

Jett nodded. "I understand."

"What brings you here?"

Glenna marveled at the bland innocence of her father's expression as if he didn't have the vaguest idea why Jett was at the inn. His face held just the right touch of curiosity and interest. She sipped her wine, wondering if Jett Coulson realized he was being bluffed.

"I'm entertaining some lobbyists from Washington." He took a swallow of straight Scotch without flinching.

"I thought I recognized some familiar faces in the lobby. That explains it," her father stated with just the right note of discovery, but Glenna was suspicious of the look Jett gave him. "I wish there were some strings they could pull for me," he sighed heavily. "The government's threatening to shut down my mine at the end of the month."

"That's too bad." The remark did not invite a further disclosure of Orin's troubles.

"Sorry, dear." Her father reached over and patted her hand. It was all Glenna could do to keep from jumping in surprise. "I promised not to bring up that subject this weekend, didn't I?"

It took her a full second to recover, during which she was careful not to look at Jett Coulson. She doubted that she was as adept as these two men were at concealing their thoughts.

"You did promise," she lied in agreement. "But I don't think I ever expected you to be able to keep it." She added the last so her father could reintroduce the subject.

"Glenna suggested this weekend excursion to distract me from the problems at the mine," her father explained. "But you're here...and the coal lobbyists. Which proves, I suppose, that a person can never run away from their problems."

"Not for long, at any rate." Jett rested his arms on the table, his silk-clad elbow brushing her forearm.

The contact swerved his gaze to her. Glenna realized why his regard was so deliciously unnerving. He looked at her as if she were the only woman in the entire room. The enigmatic glow in his dark eyes seemed to say that he knew a lot about her already, and wanted to know a lot more. His appeal was a devastating combination of virile charm and ruthless determination. Glenna could feel it slowly crumbling her resistance.

"How has your company been affected by the new government regulations?" Her father's inquiry released her from Jett's gaze. "I know you strip-mine the majority of your coal and have the Reclamation Act to contend with, but I'm referring specifically to the underground coal that can't be strip-mined."

The two men talked about mining in general for a while—its politics, new technology, and its future potential. Glenna became aware that her father was slowly steering the conversation in the direction he wanted it to take, subtly dropping facts and figures about his mine. When he nudged her with his foot, she took the hint.

She pushed her chair back from the table and smiled under Jett's questioning regard. "You and dad will probably talk 'coal' for another hour or more. In the meantime I think I'll go to my room to shower and change for dinner. If you'll excuse me."

As she rose so did Jett Coulson. At first she thought his action was prompted by courtesy until she saw him glance at his watch.

"It is getting late...and I have to change before dinner, too," he announced with casual indifference.

Glenna silently applauded the absence of frustration and disappointment on her father's face, two emotions that he had to be feeling. Instead he was smiling quite broadly.

"Well, I'm certainly not going to sit here and drink alone." Placing both hands on the table, he pushed to his feet. "I'll come with you, Glenna, and change for dinner, too."

When she noticed his legs appear wobbly from sitting for such a long time, she absently hooked an arm through her father's to give him support without it appearing that it was her purpose. Taking her time Glenna strolled in the direction of the lounge exit while she continued to help her father.

"Thank you for the drink, Orin." Jett Coulson kept pace with them. "And for the interesting conversation."

"I enjoyed talking to you," her father returned. "We'd like you to have dinner with us
tonight. You are more than welcome to join us,
if you're free."

"As I mentioned I'm entertaining guests this
weekend." As he paused his gaze strayed over
each of them. "You and your daughter are welcome to sit at my table this evening."

"We wouldn't want to intrude," Glenna was
surprised to hear her father resist the invitation.

"You won't be intruding. Everyone at the
table will probably be talking coal anyway,"
Jett shrugged.

"In that case—" her father made a pretense
of hesitating as he glanced at her "—we'll be
glad to accept."

As they left the lounge and walked to the
elevator, Jett explained that he had made
reservations to dine at eight o'clock in the for-
mal dining room. By the time they reached the
elevators, her father was steady enough on his
feet that he no longer needed Glenna's support.
She released his arm to enter the elevator first.
There wasn't any opportunity to talk during the
ride up to their floor since other guests had
crowded into the elevator, too.

When the elevator stopped at their floor, she
was surprised to discover that Jett had disem-
barked with them. She glanced at her father,
who was also frowning in bewildered astonishment.

"Is this your floor, too?" he asked.

"Yes," Jett nodded with barely a change in his expression.

"Isn't that a coincidence?" her father declared on an incredulous laugh. "It's ours, too."

"Yes, it certainly is." The dry inflection of his voice seemed to doubt it, but Glenna couldn't be sure. "I'll see you in the dining room at eight."

As he moved off down the hall, Glenna walked with her father to their adjoining suites. Suspicion reared its head, but she didn't voice it until Jett Coulson was out of hearing.

"Did you know he had a room on this floor?" she questioned.

"Of course." He unlocked his door and Glenna followed him into his suite. "Every gambler knows he has to even the odds if he can."

"Jett Coulson plays poker, too, dad."

Her remark sent a serious look chasing across his tired face. "Yes, I noticed. And he's damned good at it, too. I never once suspected that he would decide to leave when you got up to go." Then he shrugged. "It doesn't matter. I'll have another chance."

At the moment she wasn't concerned about the missed opportunity. "Why don't you rest for an hour? You have plenty of time to get ready for dinner."

"Yes, I think I'll do that." He moved woodenly toward the bed and stretched his gaunt frame atop the bed cover.

Glenna studied him for a worried second,

then unlocked the connecting door to her separate suite of rooms. She slipped quietly inside and leaned against the closed door. Had she been wrong to suggest this battle to save the mine, their home, everything? For the first time she doubted her father's ability to sway Jett Coulson onto his side.

When she dressed for dinner later that evening, she recalled her father's remark that they would go out in style. In a month they may not have a place to live, but tonight she was going to be dressed as elegantly as any woman in the room.

The jade green silk of her dress was an exotic foil to the burnished chestnut of her hair, swept atop her head in a mass of ringlets and secured by jeweled combs that had belonged to her mother. The jade material encircled her throat, leaving her shoulders and arms bare. It was nipped in tightly at the waistline, then flared into a skirt. With it she carried a crocheted shawl of silver threads.

When she knocked on the connecting door, her father was fighting with the knot of his tie. She tied it for him, noting how much good the short rest had done him. Together they went downstairs, arriving at the dining room precisely at eight o'clock. All but two of Jett's party were already there.

Glenna was aware of the curious glances she received as she was introduced to the men around the table. Their silent speculation increased when Jett seated her in a chair to his right. Her father was given the chair next to her, which put Glenna between the two men. Her position and the other guests at the table virtually negated her father's chances to talk privately with Jett.

The conversation around the dinner table was lively, focused mainly on coal as Jett had predicted. Her father included himself in the discussion quite easily. Mostly Glenna just listened to the stimulating and intelligent exchanges. She couldn't help noticing how bluntly Jett stated his opinions, never couching his replies in diplomatic terms. In contrast everyone else appeared to be the epitome of tact, phrasing their remarks so they wouldn't offend anyone.

It was a trait, she discovered, that was not limited to business discussion when Jett inquired, "Are you bored with the conversation?"

The others were busy talking and appeared unaware of the question he had addressed to Glenna. "No, I'm not bored." She lifted her gaze briefly from the prime rib she was cutting to the velvet sheen of his glance. "Dad and Bruce usually sit at the dinner table talking about daily coal production, grades and tonnage. I'm used to it."

"Bruce?" His voice carried an aloof curiosity for the identity of this unknown person.

"Bruce Hawkins," Glenna supplied the rest of his name. "He manages the mine for dad." She thought she felt his gaze boring into her, but she looked up as Jett was making a leisurely sweep of the guests.

"Does it bother you being the only female at the table?" He idly speared a piece of meat on his fork and carried it to his mouth.

Glenna let her own fork rest on the china dinner plate, bewildered by the question that had nothing to do with the subject they had previously been discussing. This confusion was reflected in her eyes.

"Why should it bother me?" she asked with a slight frown.

"I didn't say it 'should,'" he corrected smoothly. "I asked if it did."

"No, it doesn't." But she still didn't understand the point of the question.

"Perhaps you enjoy being the object of so many admiring glances?" Jett suggested.

She wasn't going to deny that she had received some. "I'm flattered, but—" Glenna didn't bother to finish the sentence, abandoning the defensive to counter. "Maybe I should ask you that first question. Does it bother you that I'm the only female at a table with all these men?"

"Not as long as you're sitting beside me it doesn't." He didn't have to hesitate over his answer, issuing it smoothly without as much as a glance in her direction.

A question from one of the other guests ended the personal conversation as Jett responded to it. The vaguely possessive ring that had been in his voice seemed to confirm that she was being singled out for his attention by this forthright and virile man. And that bothered Glenna, creating fluttering butterflies in her stomach, because she was beginning to regard him as a man rather than just as someone her father wished to do business with.

This change in attitude prompted her to notice more details about him. She studied his hard angular features, taking note of the straight bridge of his nose, the flat planes of his cheeks, his strong chin and clean jawline. On either side of his mouth arcing indentations were grooved to soften the harshness of its thin line. Sun creases fanned out from the corners of his eyes, tilting upward to emphasize the enigmatic and smiling gleam that was always in his dark eyes.

His hands and fingers were long and strong boned, but there was nothing slender or delicate about them. As Glenna watched their deft and competent movements, her imagination began weaving fantasies about their skill in a lover's caress and the sensations they might arouse on her sensitive skin. That thought was one step away from imagining the persuasive force of his mouth on hers. At that point Glenna brought her wayward thoughts to a screeching halt. No purpose would be served except to heighten her already overstimulated libido.

Distraction was provided when the dinner plates were removed and coffee was served. Jett took out a pack of cigarettes and offered one to her. She shook her head in silent refusal.

"Do you mind if I smoke?" An eyebrow was quirked in accompaniment to his question.

"I don't mind." Glenna shook her head again.

Jett started to light it, then paused to glance at her father. "Would you care for a cigarette, Orin?"

"No." His was a reluctant refusal. "The doctor made me quit smoking three years ago when I had my heart attack." But he made no mention of his recent one.

"You seem to have enjoyed a full recovery." Jett exhaled a trail of smoke, studying her father through its grayness.

Glenna was surprised to hear her father admit, "But I'm not the man I once was."

When the waiter returned a few minutes later to refill their coffee cups, a debate began among the guests whether to have more coffee or to visit the lounge for after-dinner drinks. The majority decided on the lounge, which started a general exodus from the table.

"Will you be joining us in the lounge?" Jett asked as her father courteously pulled back her chair for Glenna to stand.

The glance she exchanged with her father indicated they were both of the same mind, but he was the one who spoke. "No, thank you. It's been a long day and I need my rest."

"Thank you for dinner, Mr. Coulson," Glenna added.

"It was my pleasure."

"We enjoyed the meal. . . and the company."

Her father inserted his expression of gratitude. "Good night."

"Good night." His gaze touched each of them, lingering for a pulsing second on Glenna.

Outside the dining room Glenna and her father separated themselves from the others to walk toward the elevators. Glenna was fully aware that she possessed too much nervous energy to go to sleep yet. She would simply toss and turn if she went to bed now.

"If you don't mind, dad, I'm not coming up with you. I think I'll take a walk outside and enjoy a little of the night air before turning in," she explained.

"I certainly don't mind," he assured her. "I'll see you at breakfast in the morning."

"Good night." She brushed a kiss across his cheek, then left him to walk to a door exiting the inn.

She was nearly to the door when she saw Jett Coulson approaching. She felt the excited fluttering of her nerve ends, her pulse altering its rhythm to an uneven patter.

"Going for a stroll, Miss Reynolds?" The mildness of his tone made it less of a question and more of a complacent guess.

Glenna stopped to respond just the same. "I thought I'd walk off some of the dinner before turning in."

He paused beside her, dangerously attractive in his dark evening clothes. "That was exactly my intention. Shall we go together?"

The levelness of his gaze held a silent challenge. Alarm bells rang in her head, sending out dire warnings of the consequences in accepting. Glenna knew exactly what would happen if she took a moonlight stroll with this man. So did he. If she didn't want to know what it would be like in his arms, this was the time to say no.

"Why not?" she agreed with an expressive lift of a shoulder and returned the directness of his look.

CHAPTER FOUR

OUTSIDE the briskness of the night air prompted Glenna to lift the silver shawl to cover the bareness of her shoulders and arms from the slight chill. The touch of coolness seemed to heighten her senses, making her keenly aware of the male figure walking a scant half step behind her.

By silent consent Jett had allowed her to set the pace and the direction of their stroll. Glenna led him away from the stately white hotel onto the tree-shaded grounds. Once they had escaped the bright lights shining on the building, Glenna slowed her pace still more to wander beneath the trees.

Overhead the cloudless sky was a patchwork of stars. A misty moon sent its beams to illuminate the lawn wherever the newly leafed trees failed to shade it. Nature's creatures were offering their night songs to the breezeless air.

Glenna paused beneath a tree and leaned carefully against its rough trunk to gaze through vee openings of its branches at the sequin-studded sky. The shawl was hugged tightly around her, not in defense of the slight chill but to hold onto the enchantment of the scene.

Unbidden, the opening lines of a song came to her mind. "Almost heaven," she unconsciously murmured them aloud. The sound of her voice echoed in her ears, stirring her to the realization that she had spoken her thoughts. Straightening from the tree trunk she glanced at Jett. He was watching her, his stance relaxed. "Do you remember the song 'Country Roads'?"

"Mmm." It was an affirmative response.

Glenna wandered to the edge of the shadow the tree cast in the moonlight. The ground beneath her feet was uneven so she moved carefully.

"West Virginia is my idea of 'almost heaven,'" she explained softly while her gaze continued to admire the night sky and the soothing night sounds.

"Is it?" Jett came up behind her, stopping at a point near her right shoulder. "The slogan on the license plate is a more apt description of West Virginia—wild and wonderful. Or is that your idea of 'almost heaven?' "

She sent him a sidelong glance, angled slightly over her shoulder. "Perhaps. But I've never attempted to define it."

His head inclined slightly toward her. "What's that perfume you're wearing? That fragrance has been tantalizing me all evening."

Glenna wasn't prepared for the sudden switch of topics. Her mind raced to make the transition while her senses erupted with the intimation of his words.

"It's a new scent by Chanel. I've forgotten

the name of it." It didn't seem important as she half turned to answer him. Raw warmth spread through her in anticipation of his next move.

Glenna wasn't disappointed as his hand found the curve of her neck to tip her head back while his mouth made a steady descent to her lips. His kiss was sensually sure and softly exploring, his mouth moving back and forth across her lips with deliberate ease. Reaching out, his hand clasped her waist and turned her the rest of the way around to bring her fully into his embrace.

The warmth of his arms enfolded her, languidly heating her body with his. Under the masterful persuasion of his kiss resistance never entered her mind. The sensations he was creating within her were much too enjoyable to want them to end. This absence of force was seduction in its purest and most dangerous form.

Her eyes were closed in dreamy contentment as his mouth wandered over her cheek to the lobe of her ear. The sliding caress of his hand along her neck succeeded in pushing her shawl off one shoulder. He bent his head to let his warm lips more intimately explore the rounded bone.

"Your skin reminds me of the creamy smooth petal of a magnolia," Jett murmured against her skin, then slowly straightened.

Reluctantly Glenna raised her lashes to look at him, wishing he hadn't stopped so soon. His unfathomable black gaze wandered over her upturned face in a caressing fashion, yet managed to convey the impression that she was a very special lady.

"Why do I have the feeling that your father is setting me up for something?" It was a full moment before his casually worded question penetrated her sensually induced state of vulnerability.

Shock ran through her as Glenna realized his timing had been deliberate. Even now, while she was stiffening in his arms, his hand continued to trace the curving arc of her shoulder and neck, a thumb drawing circles on her sensitive skin. Her lips parted in a wordless and angry protest at the accusation, but her voice was temporarily lost to her.

But Jett didn't seem unduly perturbed that she failed to answer him. He continued to regard her with lazy alertness. "Your father is trying to hustle something. I haven't been able to decide whether it's his coal company... or if he's hustling you. If it's you, I might find it tempting."

When his head began a downward motion, as if to kiss her again, Glenna lashed out with her hand, slapping his face in a flash of temper. Without pausing, she pivoted out of the loose hold of his arms to stand rigid, her back to him. She expected retaliation or pursuit.

Instead Jett responded to her assault with an amused taunt. "What happened? Did I come too close to the truth?"

"No!" Swinging her head around, she denied

it too quickly and too vigorously. Instantly she realized that her anger had been born partly because Jett had so accurately seen through her father, and partly because he could think so clearly while holding her in his arms. She and her lightning-quick temper had overreacted. Bowing her head she took a calming breath.

"I lost my temper." She grudgingly offered him an apology. "I'm sorry I slapped you."

"In that case—" his voice was thick with restrained laughter as his hands reached out to turn her around and span her waist "—let's kiss and make up."

Glenna flattened her hands against his chest to brace herself away from him, but he overpowered this resistance with little effort. His hands spread up her spine to shape her to his length, the slickness of her dress offering little protection from the searing impression made by his hard muscled body.

Unable to elude his embrace, Glenna attempted verbal abuse to gain her release. "You are the most—"

His soft throaty chuckle foretold the futility of that. "I've heard all the adjectives before."

His hand cradled the back of her head to hold it still while his mouth covered her tightly compressed lips. Glenna was frustrated by the lack of brutality in his embrace. There was no punishment in his kiss, only a devouring kind of passion that ate away at her defenses. Neither was she bruised by his hands. It would have been so much easier for her to be repulsed by his embrace if he had been hurting her. Jett didn't need brute force to undermine her resistance.

When Glenna reached the point where she could no longer remain stiff in his arms and let her body become pliant against his, Jett eased his mouth from her lips. "Shall I turn the other cheek so you can slap it?"

She lowered her gaze from his sensually expert mouth to the white collar of his dress shirt, its paleness standing out sharply against the tan of his throat and the dark material of his suit. Her heartbeat was slow to return to its normal rate; so was her breathing.

"If you knew my father, you wouldn't have made the insinuation that angered me into slapping you the first time." Her voice was low, its pitch still disturbed by his kisses. "My father never 'hustled' anyone in his life."

"Perhaps 'hustle' was a bad choice of verbs," Jett conceded and loosened the enclosing circle of his arms to permit more breathing room between them. "But I know when I'm being primed."

Glenna felt a prickle of discomfort because she knew it was true. "I'm not certain that I know what you mean by that, but my father is an honest man." She could look him in the eye and say that.

"I don't recall implying that he wasn't," he returned evenly and let his gaze run over her face. "Mainly I'm curious what part you play in his plans."

"None. I'm just here if he needs me," Glenna

shrugged because moral support was the limit of
her involvement. She had never taken an active
part in his business affairs. It would be a poor
time to become involved now when skillful
negotiations were required, and she was a
bungling amateur.

Jett didn't appear totally convinced by her
reply, but seemed willing to withhold judgment.
The corners of his mouth deepened in a dry
smile as his arms slid from her to let her stand
free.

"Do you think he will need you?" he
mused.

Without the warmth of his body heat, Glenna
shivered. She was beyond coping with his
double-edged questions. "It's getting cool. I
think I'll go in now."

If she expected a protest from Jett there was
none forthcoming. "I'll walk with you."

They retraced their path to the inn in silence.
He stayed at her side until she reached the
elevator. He saw her safely inside and punched
the button to her floor.

"Good night, Glenna." He used her given
name easily, but she didn't have time to
reciprocate before the doors slid closed.

In her room Glenna knocked once on the connecting door to her father's suite. There was
only silence on the other side. She hesitated,
then opened the door to look in. She tiptoed to
the bed where her father was sleeping peaceful-
ly, so she didn't waken him. It was a while
before she fell asleep.

THE RINGING of the telephone wakened her the next morning. She groped blindly for the receiver as she tried to shake the sleep from her senses.

"Yes?" Her voice sounded as thick as her tongue felt.

"Wake up, sleepyhead," her father's cheerful voice admonished. "Rise and shine."

Glenna let her head fall back on the pillow while managing to keep the phone to her ear. "What time is it?" She frowned drowsily.

"Eight A.M."

"Why did you call me? Why didn't you just knock on the door?" She sat up in bed and rubbed her eyes, trying to wipe the sleep out of them.

"I'm downstairs, that's why. I've been up for a couple of hours, took an early morning stroll. I thought I might run into Coulson, but I understand he ordered breakfast in his room." The reference to Jett blinked Glenna's eyes open wide with the memory of last night. "Are you going to join me for breakfast or do I have to eat alone?"

"I'll be down, but dad...." Glenna hesitated. "Don't try to see Jett until I've had a chance to talk to you."

"Why?" There was a puzzled note in his voice.

"I'll explain it all when I come down. Just give me a few minutes to wash my face and get dressed."

In all it took Glenna a fast twenty minutes to

wash, put on fresh makeup, and don a pair of
wheat-tan slacks with a matching knit top in
narrow stripes of cream and tan. Her father was
already seated at a table when she joined him in
the restaurant for breakfast.

"What did you mean on the phone? Why do
you need to talk to me?" her father queried almost before she had scotted her chair up to the
table.

Briefly Glenna explained about Jett accom-
panying her on the walk last night, leaving out
the intimate details of the kiss. "He suspects
that you're setting him up for something," she
concluded.

"He said that?" A troubled frown puckered
his brow.

"To be precise, he said he knew he was being
primed."

"Mmm." Orin Reynolds thought for a moment. "I don't want him to get the impression
that I'm some kind of shyster, so I'll have to be
more direct with him. Otherwise he won't
believe that I want to make a legitimate business
proposition."

"That's what I felt," she agreed.

"I had hoped to get on friendlier terms with
him before making my proposal, but that's
out," he sighed, then sent her a thin smile.
"Thanks for the warning."

The waitress came to take their orders, but her
arrival didn't affect their conversation. They had
already finished their discussion. It was a quiet
meal with her father lost in his own thoughts

There wasn't any sign of Jett around the hotel that morning. They didn't see him until lunchtime when they were seated at a table in the restaurant. Glenna saw him enter the room and managed a whispered, "Dad," to draw her father's attention to the tall black-haired man approaching their table.

"Good afternoon." Jett's greeting encompassed both of them, a greeting that they echoed. Without any further preliminaries, he rested a hand on the back of Glenna's chair and leaned the other one on the table to face her at right angles. That caressing and intense look was in his eyes that made her feel she was someone special as he directed all of his attention to her. "Would you like to play a game of tennis this afternoon? I have a court reserved for two o'clock."

His closeness had a heady effect on her. She glanced at her father to escape the spell Jett was casting over her. Her father mistook the glance, believing that she was seeking his permission.

"Go ahead and enjoy yourself. I'll find something to keep me amused," he insisted.

"Two o'clock then." Jett repeated the time in confirmation of her decision.

"I'll be there." Glenna nodded.

As Jett straightened to leave her father spoke up. "There is a business matter I would like to discuss with you when you have time."

Jett eyed her father with a knowing half-smile. "I would be available at four-thirty, if that suits you."

"It's fine." There was a wealth of confidence in Orin Reynolds's expression, every bit equal to Jett's. "My suite or yours."

"Yours."

Glenna remembered, "I don't have a tennis racket."

"I'll get one for you," Jett promised and moved away with a waving flick of his hand. He walked over to join two men that Glenna recognized as having attended the dinner the previous night, obviously two of his guests.

"Well, all my cards will be spread on the table by five this afternoon," her father stated with a resigned sigh.

"What do you think he will do?" Glenna picked up her glass of ice water and sipped at it to cool the heat coursing through her veins, all the while keeping track of Jett's movements over the rim of her glass.

"That is one man I wouldn't begin to second-guess," her father declared and crumpled the linen cloth protecting his lap, depositing it on the tabletop. "If you are ready to leave, I am."

Glenna's answer was to push her chair back and stand up. After they had left the restaurant they returned to their suite of rooms so Glenna could change into her tennis clothes. She could hear her father prowling around in his adjoining room, alternately sitting and pacing. His tension become contagious. Everything they had rested on the outcome of his meeting with Jett this afternoon.

Wearing a white headband to keep the hair

out of her eyes, she arrived at the tennis courts. Jett was waiting for her. He gestured to a trio of rackets. "Take your pick."

She tried each of them before choosing the second one. Her nerves felt as taut as the racket strings, a combination of apprehension for their financial situation and the increasing havoc Jett was raising with her senses.

When they had taken the court Glenna agreed with his suggestion to loosen up with a few practice volleys. Usually she was an above-average player, but she was lacking concentration. In consequence she started out playing badly.

Halfway through the first set Glenna hadn't scored once. What was more damning to her pride was the knowledge that Jett was not trying to score. When she managed to get her serve in, he returned it and kept a slow volley going, never trying for a crosscourt or baseline. On her last serve she double-faulted to give him set point.

Angry with herself for playing so poorly, and with him for being so condescending, Glenna barely glanced at him when they switched ends. But he goaded her in passing.

"You'd better get your mind on the game. Your problem is you're not concentrating."

The criticism was a stinging prod. Glenna returned his first serve with a blistering crosscourt shot that caught him flat-footed. From that point on her game improved. Yet she was never equal to Jett. He would let her draw close, even win a game or two, but each time the match was in jeopardy, he'd slam home a shot that she couldn't return.

The strong competitive streak within Glenna refused to let her quit. Jett was controlling the game, running her legs off, but she kept battling until he won the match point. Perspiration ran in rivulets down her neck as she walked in defeat toward the net. Winded, she was gripping her side while he vaulted the net, barely out of breath.

"Congratulations." The handshake she offered him was limp, as exhausted as her voice.

"Tired?" There was a taunting smile in his tone.

Resentment flared wearily in her gray green eyes as she wiped her forehead with the back of her hand. Turning, she walked slowly off the court, aware that Jett fell in step with her.

"You could have annihilated me," she accused. "Wiped me off the court anytime you wanted. I don't like the idea that you were just toying with me, playing cat and mouse."

"It seemed more of a contest, didn't it?" he handed her a towel.

"I don't think you even worked up a sweat," Glenna complained, her voice partially muffled by the towel she used to wipe her face.

"I did," he assured her on a lazy note. "You are a pretty good player when you concentrate."

"No mouse likes to be patronized." She draped the towel around her neck, letting the ends hang down the front.

"I have never seen a mouse with chestnut hair before or a temper to match it," Jett chided with a wicked glint in his eye.

Her breath had returned to a more even rate. She lifted her head to look at him. "I'm not really a sore loser, although it might sound like that. It's just that... being allowed to come close is almost as bad as being allowed to win," she explained. "What satisfaction is there if you know someone *let* you do it?"

"You have a valid point." His hands caught the ends of her towel, pulling her closer to him. With each breath she inhaled his earthy male scent, heightened by perspiration and the heat of exertion. It did funny things to her pulse. "But it wasn't my intention to appear patronizing. You are a fierce competitor. I felt you were entitled to some kind of reward for your efforts. You just wouldn't give up."

"I never quit." It was unthinkable.

Jett wiped her cheek with an end of her towel, managing to give the impression of a caress. "I realize that."

Then his hand was under her chin, lifting it so his mouth could claim her lips. Glenna tasted the salty flavor of him in the moist union of their lips as she swayed against the hard support of his length. She was still thirsting for more of his kisses when he slowly drew away from her clinging lips.

"I suppose you mentioned to your father what we discussed last night. Is that why he asked to meet me this afternoon?" Jett murmured.

Dammit! He was doing it again. Catching her off guard with her senses drugged by the potency of his kisses. Glenna straightened from him, containing her anger with an effort.

"Yes, I told him about your misguided suspicions," she admitted since there wasn't any point in lying. "I think he wants to meet you to correct the impression you were forming about him."

"What does he want to talk to me about?" Jett continued to watch her while he slipped his tennis racket into its protective carrying case.

"Dad could explain it better than I can." Glenna didn't try to convince him that she didn't know. "I told you before I'm not involved with any of his business affairs."

"Then it is about business?" He requested confirmation of the subject matter.

"Yes." It was a clipped response. She picked up the tennis racket she had used, holding it in an attitude of indecision. "What am I supposed to do with this?" Glenna made a subconscious attempt to divert the conversation.

Jett motioned to an attendant. "He'll return it." Glenna handed it to the young boy who jogged over. As soon as he'd left Jett asked, "Will you be at the meeting?"

"Probably. Why?" She tried to challenge him.

"I just wondered." With a hand resting on

the small of her back, he guided her away from the tennis courts.

Glenna was wary of such a noncommittal answer. "What did you wonder?"

His sidelong glance held her gaze for a moment. "If you were a shill."

"A shill," she repeated in growing indignation.

"A shill is a gambling term. It refers to a partner, a decoy used to dupe the victims into a game—usually a crooked game," he explained.

"I know what it means," Glenna retorted. "But I don't happen to be one."

"It's possible that your purpose could be to divert my attention. You are a very attractive diversion." His glance was swiftly assessing.

Glenna didn't trust herself to look at him, certain she would strike at him again. "But that isn't my purpose."

"So you said," he nodded.

"You really have a very suspicious mind," she stated in a low angry breath. "Does everybody have to have an angle, some ulterior motive?"

"They don't have to but they usually do." His delivery was smoothly offhand, but there was a wealth of cynicism in his words.

"Maybe it's because you do most of your business with underhanded people instead of honest ones like my father," Glenna suggested dryly.

"Get burned a few times, and you'll get leery of fire, too."

Her gaze slid to his face, noting the grimness of his mouth and the forbidding set of his jaw. Glenna realized that his toughness, his hardness came from harsh experience. It lessened her irritation.

"I don't have to be at the meeting," she pointed out. "If it would make you feel more secure, or less suspicious, I'll go for a swim or something. There isn't anything I can contribute to the discussion. And I certainly don't want you to regard me as a distraction. Neither would dad."

As they stopped in front of the elevators, Jett studied her for a long second before commenting on her suggestion. "I have no objection to your presence at the meeting with your father. If you want to attend, you can."

"If it's up to me, I'll be there." Because she knew her presence would provide moral support for her father, which was of greater importance than Jett's distrust.

The elevator doors slid soundlessly open as a bell chimed overhead. Glenna stepped to one side to let its passengers walk by her before entering the empty elevator ahead of Jett.

CHAPTER FIVE

THE MEETING was a nerve-racking experience for Glenna. She was curled in a chair off to one side, trying to be as unobtrusive as possible. Her father had begun the meeting by first establishing the profitability of the mine, producing studies and reports for Jett's examination. From there he had gone on to explain previous years' financial difficulties, then the inspection order for safety improvements and the long appeals in order to raise the money to comply with the required standards.

All the while Jett had listened, looked over the papers and reports, and studied the man doing the talking. And all the while his face had been devoid of expression. Never once had he glanced at Glenna since greeting her shortly after he had arrived. She shifted in her chair to ease a cramped leg, yet the movement didn't attract his attention.

"I think that gives you a fairly good idea of my present dilemma." Her father leaned back in his chair to study Jett and try to read his reaction. After an instant's pause he laid out his proposal. "And why I am anxious to form an association...a merger with your firm, to obtain the financial strength I need."

Jett glanced over a report in his hand before leaning forward to set it on the table atop others. "You have explained that your credit has been overextended because of recent economic reversals in the industry. While your operation can't be classified as lucrative, it appears to be stable. Lending institutions have made loans on less strength than what you've shown me. Their reason for refusing you can't be based on your indebtedness or lack of collateral. What was it?" There was something very casual and indifferent about the way Jett shook out a cigarette from its pack and lighted it.

"As you know, a single-mine owner is in a precarious position. He virtually has a one-man operation. If something happens to that one man, there is no operation. On the other hand—" her father shrugged "—your company is made up of a team of men. If something happens to one of them, you replace him, but the loss of one man does not jeopardize your company's existence."

"True," Jett agreed and waited for him to continue.

As Glenna studied her father she noticed the tightening of his mouth. She was well aware of the effort it took for her father to finish his explanation.

"In the last three years I've had two heart attacks. A year from now I may not be here. That's why I can't get a loan," he explained.

"If I'm gone, who would run the mine? Glenna certainly couldn't. Not because she's a woman. Her skills happen to be in another field. Without me there's no one to run the operation and make sure the debts are paid."

His statement prompted a question that Glenna unwittingly offered aloud. "What about Bruce?"

Tired gray eyes sent her a rueful look. "Bruce is a competent individual when he has someone to give him directions. He's a stopgap, capable of holding things together alone only over a short period of time," he explained to both her and Jett.

Her gaze was magnetically drawn to Jett. He was eyeing her with quiet contemplation, but she was struck by the emotionless set of his features. When his gaze broke contact with hers, it was to slide downward and linger on the soft outline of her lips. This betrayal of interest was the first he'd shown toward her. It was quickly gone as his attention reverted to her father.

"Without this merger I stand to lose a great deal," Orin said, which was an understatement. "But I'm not the only one who would suffer. The economy of our small community has barely recovered from the last shutdown. I don't know how many could survive if the mine is closed again for an extended period of time."

"I can appreciate what you are saying." Jett exhaled a stream of smoke and tapped his cigarette in an ashtray.

"Naturally I don't have to point out to you the tax advantages your company would enjoy by absorbing my operation. I wouldn't even make this proposition if there wasn't a way you could benefit from it," her father insisted, then paused as if suddenly realizing he had no more arguments to make. "I don't expect you to give me an answer right away. You need time to consider it."

"If I may, I'd like to take a copy of the reports you've shown me so I can go over them." He gestured toward the papers on the table.

"You can take those," her father offered.

"Between tonight and tomorrow I'll have a chance to study them." When Jett uncoiled his length to stand, it signaled an end to the meeting. Whatever followed was merely a formality. "I'll let you know tomorrow afternoon whether I think your proposal is something my company would wish to pursue."

"That sounds fair enough to me." Orin rose with difficulty to shake hands.

Glenna stood, too, as Jett picked up the stack of reports. Her gaze searched his face, but whatever opinion he had, he was keeping it strictly to himself. With a nodded farewell in her direction, he let her father escort him to the door.

When the door was closed behind him, her father turned back to the center of the room, glanced at Glenna, and sighed heavily. "We only have twenty-four more hours to wait before we have a decision. At least we won't be kept dangling for days."

"Excuse me, dad." She hurried to the door that Jett had just exited. "I'll be right back."

"Where are you going?" He blinked in confusion.

"I just want to have a word with him for a minute," Glenna rushed and disappeared into the hallway. She walked swiftly, the poise of maturity giving her an air of confidence. In the corridor ahead of her she saw him opening the door to his suite. "Jett." The firm ring of her voice requested him to wait for her. He paused on the threshold of his suite, an eyebrow slightly quirked in silent inquiry and speculation.

As soon as she reached him Jett entered his suite, sending an invitation over his shoulder for her, "Come in." From the doorway Glenna noticed a second person in the sitting room of Jett's suite. A conservative suit and tie covered his portly figure. His balding head made the man appear considerably older than she suspected he was. When he saw Glenna following Jett into the suite he stood up quickly, self-consciously smoothing his tie down the front of his protruding stomach and trying not to show his surprise.

"This is Don Sullivan," Jett introduced the man in an offhand manner. "He works for me in an organizational capacity. Don, meet Glenna Reynolds."

"How do you do, Mr. Sullivan," Glenna murmured as the man bobbed his head in her direction with faint embarrassment. She bit at the inside of her lip, wondering how she was going to speak to Jett alone.

But he was already arranging it. "Would you mind stepping into the other room for a few minutes, Don?" It was an order, phrased as a question. Before the man could take a step, Jett was handing him the reports her father had let him take. "I want you to look these over, too, so we can discuss them later."

"I will." Again the man bobbed his head at Glenna as he moved his stocky frame toward an inner door.

When it was closed and they were alone Jett turned slowly to meet Glenna's steady look. "You wanted to speak to me?"

"My father told you the whole truth. He didn't leave anything out," she said evenly. "I wanted to be sure you knew that, considering how suspicious you have been."

"I ran a check on your father. The report came back before I met with him this afternoon," he stated. "So I was already familiar with his present situation."

"Then why didn't you let him know?" Glenna frowned.

"If your father is the businessman that I think he is, he has already guessed that I had him checked out. He would have done the same thing in my place." Jett picked up a sheaf of papers that Don Sullivan had been working on when they had come in, and glanced through them.

The implied compliment for her father eased

some of her tension. "Then you do believe he is honest."

"Your father mentioned two negative facts that I had no information about. . .and would probably have had difficulty obtaining. So, yes, I believe he gave me a fair picture." He replaced the loose papers on the table where he'd found them and allowed a faint smile to touch his mouth when he looked at Glenna. "Does that reassure you?"

"Yes." There was an inward sigh as that possible prejudice had been eliminated. A noise in the adjoining room reminded her of the man waiting for him. She took a step toward the hall door. "I won't keep you any longer."

"What? Aren't you going to add your voice to your father's appeal?" A gentle mockery gleamed in his dark eyes, taunting but not cruelly so.

"Would it do any good?" Glenna countered in light challenge.

"It might prove entertaining," he replied with a raking look that was deliberately suggestive. Then his expression sobered. "I will consider it as seriously as I would any business proposition."

Glenna didn't feel she could expect more than that. "Thank you," she murmured and left the room to return to her father's suite.

Despite the reassurance from Jett, the waiting for his decision was difficult, both for Glenna and her father. Throughout the evening she wavered between a certainty that Jett would agree and a cold fear that he would not.

She slept restlessly, waking with the first glint of dawn. After lying in bed for nearly an hour trying to go back to sleep, Glenna climbed out of bed and dressed in a pair of dark blue slacks and a cream white velour sweater. It was half-past five when she ventured into the corridor to take the elevator downstairs.

In the hotel lobby Glenna skirted the restaurant with its aroma of fresh-perked coffee in favor of the invigorating crispness of the early morning air, seeking its quiet serenity to soothe her troubled mind. She wandered through the dew-wet grounds with no particular destination in mind, yet aware her steps were taking her in the general direction of the stables.

For a while it seemed she had it all to herself, sharing the yellow morning only with the twittering birds in the trees, until she noticed a man strolling alongside an inn road. She recognized Jett immediately, her pulses quickening. Her meandering path intersected the road, and she turned onto it to walk toward him, neither hurrying her pace nor slowing it.

As she drew closer, she saw that he was dressed in his evening clothes—or had been. The tie was unknotted and hanging loosely around his neck, the top buttons of his white shirt unfastened. His suit jacket was slung over one shoulder, held by the hook of his finger, and his sharply creased slacks looked wrinkled. There was even a dusty film dulling the polished sheen of his black shoes.

"If you are just coming in, it must have been some party," Glenna remarked when Jett was within hearing. "What happened? Did you decide to go horseback riding at midnight and get thrown?"

"No, I haven't been riding. Only walking," he corrected dryly, both stopping when only two feet separated them. "You're an early bird this morning."

"I couldn't go back to sleep so I got up." Her gray green eyes inspected the weary lines in his face and the rumpled blackness of his thick hair. "Haven't you been to bed?"

"No. After dinner I went over some business with Don. It was around two A.M. before he left the suite. I went for a walk out in the hills to do some thinking, and stayed around to watch the sun come up." His features took on a faraway look when he partially glanced over his shoulder in the general direction he'd just come from.

Glenna leaned toward him, reading something in his expression that gripped her throat. "Have you decided about the merger?" she asked tightly.

His gaze glided to her face, moving over it for an instant, the line of his mouth slanting. "I'll give your father my answer this afternoon." He deftly avoided the question.

"Are you still considering it?" A breeze came whirling out of the trees to blow across her face, briefly lifting the chestnut hair away from her neck before it danced away.

Jett rested a heavy hand atop her shoulder. "There is a lot to consider, Glenna."

"I'm sure there is," she agreed on a subdued note, lowering her gaze to the front of his shirt. "It's just the waiting to find out that's so hard."

"All decisions are hard. Life is hard." His voice was gentle, but the grip of his hand applied pressure to her shoulder bone, drawing her half a step closer. He swung his jacket behind her in order to lock both his hands behind her neck. "It would have been easy if you had been the one to suggest a merger with me." The seductive pitch of his voice made it plain that he had something much more intimate in mind than a business liaison. "You present a very attractive package."

Glenna was conscious that he had bent his head toward her, but she didn't lift her gaze. If he was trying to divert her thoughts from her father, he was succeeding with his closeness. The flattery wasn't necessary.

"You didn't have to say that. I don't need to be sweet-talked out of asking questions about your decision. I can accept the fact that you haven't made up your mind," she told him.

"Glenna, I never say anything I don't mean." The firmness of his tone enforced his statement, compelling her to tip her head up to examine his face.

There were still signs of tiredness and lack of

sleep etched in his features, but the smoldering intensity of his eyes shallowed out her breathing. Jett eliminated the last few inches to claim her curving mouth while his hands slid down her back to enfold her in his arms.

Her senses erupted with a wonderful rawness that needed his embrace to soothe it. Everywhere her body came in contact with his muscled frame a wild current seemed to flow between them—a current that spread its tingling pleasure through the rest of her flesh. The ache of passion knotted her abdomen. Its sudden presence tempered the ardency of her response until she regained control of her senses to end the kiss.

She had always been cognizant of the sexual attraction Jett had aroused, but their previous kisses had not led her to expect this flaming leap into desire. It shook her. Glenna felt the weakness in her knees and didn't try to immediately move away from him. Her hands were spread across his shirt front. Beneath them she could feel the thudding of his heartbeat, its tempo disturbed like hers was.

"Your volatility isn't limited to your temper, is it?" Jett mused.

"I don't know what happened. I—" Glenna half turned, self-conscious and unnerved.

"Hey, I'm not complaining," he chuckled and caught at her hand, clasping it warmly within his fingers. "That looks like a comfortable tree. Why don't we sit down, rest a little before making the long walk back to the hotel?'' He led her toward a large tree on the lawn.

"The grass is wet," she pointed out, the green blades of grass glistening with the sheen of dew. Jett solved that problem by spreading his suit jacket on the grass. "It'll get grass stains on it."

"So? I'll send it to the cleaners." He lowered himself to the ground and pulled Glenna down beside him on the other half of his jacket. The trunk of the tree served as a backrest for him, but it wasn't wide enough for Glenna to lean against it, too. Instead Jett shifted her so she was resting diagonally across his chest, his arms overlapping around her waist. "Mmm." He nuzzled the curve of her neck. "Maybe I couldn't sleep last night because I was missing this," he suggested.

The stubble of his beard growth was pleasantly rough against her sensitive skin. It conveyed the rasping caress of a cat's tongue as he rubbed his chin and jaw along her neck. The hard support of his chest and arms, and the pressure of his hipbone began to embed themselves on her flesh. Glenna felt herself slipping again into that mindless oblivion of sensation. She changed her position to elude the mouth exploring the sensitive hollow behind her ear, turning sideways in his arms to rest a shoulder against his chest.

"Is something wrong?" Jett cupped a hand to her cheek, tipping her head so he could inspect her face.

"Not really." It seemed impossible that she had only known him for two days. The angled planes of his features seemed so very familiar to her. It was just that the pace of their relationship had just accelerated, and Glenna wanted to slow it down before it carried her away.

His hand idly left her face to reach down to lift her left hand. His gaze studied the bareness of her fingers, his thumb running over the tops of them. When he lifted his gaze there was interest, curiosity, and the banked flame of desire gleaming in his look.

"No rings," Jett observed. "Have there ever been any?"

"If you mean, have I ever been married? No," she replied with a slight shake of her head.

"Engaged?"

"No." The latent sexiness of his look was having a chaotic effect on her pulse.

"How old are you?" Jett continued with his questions.

"Twenty-four."

"No steady boyfriends?"

"None." At the skeptical lift of his eyebrow, Glenna qualified her answer. "Not unless you count Bruce."

"Bruce Hawkins. The man who manages the mine for your father?" His recognition of the name was instant. He asked only for her confirmation.

"Yes. Bruce and I have become close friends since my father had his first attack. Since dad has to restrict his activities, Bruce comes to the house a lot to discuss things with him," she explained.

"He's been like a brother to you then, another member of the family," he deduced.

"Something like that," Glenna agreed.

His hand continued to massage her fingers, rubbing them in a sensuous manner that aroused all sorts of tremors. "Do you think he regards you as a sister?"

She started to say yes, but when she met his knowing look she knew that wasn't true. After a pause she admitted, "I don't think so."

"Neither do I."

Jett released her hand to let his fingers seek the mass of hair at the back of her head. By the time Glenna realized his intention she had lost the will to resist. The searing possession of his mouth parted her lips to deepen the kiss with the intimacy of his exploring tongue. Hot flames shot through her veins, melting her bones and burning her flesh with a feverish heat.

Her hand slid under his arm to circle the back of his waist, her fingers spreading over the taut muscles of his spine. When he uncombed his fingers from her hair, he cradled her head on the flexed muscle of his upper arm. She let her fingers glide up the front of his shirt to slide inside his collar, discovering the exhilarating feel of his tanned throat beneath her hand and the wild tattoo of the vein in his neck.

Glenna shuddered with intense longing. The quiver continued when she felt the touch of his fingers pushing their way under her sweater to the bare skin over her rib cage. The breath she took became lodged somewhere, time standing still as he cupped a ripe breast in the circling cradle of his hand.

Through the spinning recesses of her mind a voice came to ask if what she felt was real. Or whether it was simply natural desire that had been suppressed too long and was now being uncovered by an expert. Her conscience rejected sexual involvement with the accompaniment of emotion.

Trembling, but with growing strength, Glenna began to strain away from his drugging kiss. At the first sign of resistance Jett began to seek control of his own passion, not attempting to overpower her.

When he lifted his head, both were breathing raggedly. Glenna sat up, shakily tucking a strand of auburn hair behind her ear. Silence stretched between them for several seconds. Then Jett rolled to his feet and held out a hand to pull her upright.

"Have you had breakfast?" he asked when she was standing.

"No. I wasn't very hungry." She watched him bend to scoop up his suit jacket. "I thought the fresh air might wake up my appetite."

"Are you hungry now?" His fingertips touched her elbow to start her in the direction of the inn.

"A little."

"For food?" His downward glance noted the very faint blush in her cheeks. "I guess I didn't have to say the obvious, did I?"

"No."

"Glenna."

Something in his voice raised her head. He was looking at her with an intensity that she found a little frightening.

"What?" she prompted when he didn't immediately speak.

A tiny frown appeared between his eyebrows as his gaze swung to the front. "Never mind. It wasn't important." He seemed suddenly very remote. Lifting a hand, he rubbed the side of his jaw. "I need a shave...and some sleep."

There didn't seem to be any comment for Glenna to make, so she fell into an uneasy silence. Jett made no attempt to break it during the walk back to the inn. Shortly after they had entered the lobby Glenna spied her father.

"There you are, Glenna." He hurried toward them. "I wondered where you were. Have you had breakfast?" A frown clouded his expression when he recognized Jett and took in his slightly disheveled appearance. "Good morning, Jett."

"Good morning, Orin," he replied and immediately excused himself. "I'll talk with both of you later today."

It was left to Glenna to explain, as Jett walked to the elevators, how she had come to meet him.

CHAPTER SIX

GLENNA GLANCED AT HER WATCH for the fifth time in the last five minutes. Irritated that so little time had passed she turned and retraced her path to the window overlooking the front grounds of the inn. It was the same view of trees and grass and driveway. She pivoted away to wander back toward the door of the suite.

"You are going to wear a hole in the carpet if you keep walking back and forth in the same place," her father complained, chiding her in a paternal fashion while he drummed his fingers on the armrest of his chair.

"You aren't exactly a picture of serenity," Glenna retorted dryly.

"No, I suppose I'm not," he admitted, releasing a long breath.

"Maybe I should call him," she suggested. "He might not realize we're waiting for him. There wasn't any specific time mentioned."

"Coulson knows we're waiting to hear from him," he assured her. "He'll be here...sooner or later."

But could her nerves stand the "later"? Glenna threaded her fingers together, squeezing them tightly while she tried to ignore the tension churning her stomach. Restlessly her gaze searched the room for some object to distract her attention from the endless waiting.

A sharp knock at the door snapped the fragile thread of her control. She whirled toward the sound, then paused to meet her father's glance. He drew in a deep breath and forced a grim smile on his mouth. Taking his lead, Glenna gathered together her composure before forcing herself to walk sedately to the door.

Turning the knob, she stepped to one side as she opened it to admit Jett. She struggled to behave normally when she met the blandness of his gaze. She even managed a smile of welcome.

"Sorry I kept you waiting. I was delayed or I would have been here sooner," Jett explained smoothly, pausing while Glenna closed the door behind him. "I received a long-distance phone call just as I was about to leave."

"It couldn't be helped." She accepted his apology while her gaze searched the impenetrable mask of his features. "You look rested. Did you get some sleep?" she asked conversationally as they walked the rest of the way into the room where her father was seated.

"A couple of hours."

Her alert gaze had already noted his smoothly shaven face and the starched crispness of his striped shirt and charcoal slacks. With him, Jett had the reports her father had given him the previous afternoon. Yet, more than the freshness of his appearance, Glenna noticed the coolness of his attitude. The pleasantness was all on the surface. A chill ran up her spine as she darted a look at her father.

When Jett walked over to set the reports on the table beside his chair her father said—quite calmly, "It's no, isn't it?"

Her gaze raced to Jett in a silent plea for her father to be wrong, but Jett didn't glance at her. He met the pair of gray eyes squarely, without a flicker of regret.

"No." It was a flat refusal.

Glenna nearly choked on the bitter taste of defeat, but she didn't make a sound. Her personal disappointment was fleeting. If the announcement was a crushing blow to her, it had to be much more severe for her father. It was his life's work that was being lost. Her heart swelled with pride at the stoic acceptance he was displaying over Jett's decision.

"Very well," he nodded. "It was worth a try."

"May I ask why you turned down his proposal?" Glenna felt her voice sounded quite calm, with only a trace of rawness in its tone.

"It's quite simple." The piercing blackness of his gaze was turned to her. "If my company is interested in acquiring your mine, it would be much more economical to let him go broke. A merger would mean assuming all of his debts and liabilities as well as his assets. Those debts are more than the mine is worth. Which wipes out the tax savings. Therefore the merger isn't to our advantage."

"I understand." Despite her outward com-

posure, inside she was raging at his coldly
logical reasoning that didn't take any human
factor into account.

As if reading her mind his gaze narrowed.
"Your father would be the only one who would
really benefit from the merger. And Coulson
Mining is not a charitable institution." He
turned back to her father. "This was strictly a
business matter. I had to make a business decision." It was a flat statement with no apology
for the outcome.

"I understand perfectly," her father replied.
"I didn't want you to regard it in any other
manner."

There was a second's pause before Jett extended an arm to shake her father's hand. "I
wish you luck, Orin."

"A gambler can always use some of that." A
wan smile pulled at the corners of her father's
mouth in a weak attempt at humor.

After he had released her father's hand, his
gaze rested for a scant instant on Glenna. Then
he crossed the room to the door and left without
another word.

His departure released the paralysis that had
gripped her limbs. Glenna moved to her father's
chair, wanting to comfort him and wanting to
be comforted herself. She reached out to tenta-
tively rest a hand on his shoulder, worried by
the lack of expression in his face. He patted her
hand almost absently.

"We'll figure something out, daddy." Unconsciously she used the term "daddy" instead

of dad. She hadn't called him that since she was a child.

"No, we've lost it. The mine, the house, everything," he declared on a hollow note, staring off into space. "If a merger wasn't profitable for Coulson, there isn't anyone else who can help us. I'm through. Finished."

"Don't say that, daddy." She knelt beside his chair, fighting the tears that were making the huge lump in her throat. "You are a Reynolds, remember? We never quit."

He didn't seem to hear her. She searched wildly through her mind for some alternative, some other way to save everything, but there was only blankness.

"I'm tired, Glenna," he said after several minutes. His eyes appeared empty when he looked at her. "I think I'll lie down for a while. Will you help me up?"

The request frightened her as nothing else had. He had always been too proud to ask for help, or to admit he needed it before. His pride was broken. Glenna felt she was picking up the pieces when she slipped an arm around him to help him out of the chair. She walked with him to his bed and spread the light coverlet over him.

"You'll feel better after you rest," she insisted in an effort to reassure herself. "Later on we'll call room service and order steak and champagne. We're going to go out in style, remember, dad?"

"I don't think I'll feel like eating tonight." He closed his eyes.

Glenna stared at him, then finally pulled up a chair beside his bed. He appeared to sleep. She remained near him, worried about his heart and wanting to be there if he became ill.

At seven o'clock she had a sandwich sent up for herself and a bowl of soup for her father. She was partially reassured when he wakened and voluntarily sat up to eat the soup. He continued to be withdrawn, unresponsive to her attempts at conversation, but the leadenness of depression had left his eyes. She turned on the television for a while until he announced that he wanted to go to bed. Leaving the connecting door ajar, Glenna returned to her own suite.

CHAPTER SEVEN

MECHANICALLY, Glenna changed out of her clothes into her turquoise green nightgown and matching satin robe. Too many things were running through her mind, leaving no room to think of sleep. She moved restlessly around the room, slipping in to check on her father half a dozen times.

Her head was pounding with the effort to find a solution. Two thoughts kept reoccurring in her mind. One was her father's insistence that Jett Coulson had been their only possible source of help. The second was the remark Jett had made to her early that morning about how easy his decision would have been if she had wanted a merger with him.

Pressing a hand to her forehead, Glenna tried to rationally think out her problem. Jett was attracted to her. That was an indisputable fact. He had made his decision on a purely business basis, but what if she appealed to him on a personal level? How much influence did she have? Could she persuade him to reconsider?

When the barrage of silent questions stopped, a calmness settled over her. She had to find out. For the sake of her father, she had to try. With a course of action chosen, Glenna moved to carry it out.

The hotel corridor was empty when she ventured into it. She walked swiftly to the door of Jett's suite and knocked lightly on it. Only at that second did she consider the possibility that he might not be alone—or that he might not even be there. The turning of the latch eliminated the last. When Jett opened the door a glance past him found no one else in the sitting room.

He stood in the opening, one hand holding the door and the other resting on the frame. Under the steadiness of his gaze, Glenna couldn't find her voice. Taking his time, he let his gaze travel over the draping fabric of her robe as it outlined the jutting curves of her breasts and hips. In a strictly defensive reaction to his visual assault, her hand moved to finger the satin ribbon that secured the front of her robe.

Without saying a word Jett opened the door wider and moved out of the way. Her hesitation was brief before she glided past him into the sitting room. She pivoted around to face him when she heard the click of the door latch. He was wearing the same pale gray striped shirt he'd had on this afternoon, but the sleeves were rolled up to expose his tanned forearms.

"It occurred to me that you might come to see me." Instead of walking to her, he went to a table strewn with papers that he'd obviously been working on, and half sat on the edge.

"Then you know why I'm here." Her voice came out husky.

There was a pack of cigarettes amid the stacks of papers. Jett removed one from the pack and lighted it. "You came to see if you couldn't persuade me to reconsider your father's proposal." He sounded so distant that Glenna unconsciously moved closer to him.

"Is it so much to ask, Jett?" she questioned. "My father has everything at stake. His whole life's work."

"A good gambler keeps an ace up his sleeve. I wondered if your father was going to play his ace of hearts." He studied her through the smoke screen of his burning cigarette.

"Ace of hearts? Are you referring to me?" Glenna frowned, confused by his attitude. "My father doesn't know I'm here."

"He didn't send you?" An eyebrow was arched in question.

"He's in his room, sleeping. He has no idea that I'm here. If he knew—" When she imagined her father's reaction, she averted her glance from Jett. "He wouldn't approve."

"Then this was all your idea," Jett concluded.

"Yes." She watched as he reached across the table for a half-filled ashtray. With one hip on the edge of the table and his other leg braced in front of him, he held the ashtray in the palm of his hand, the forearm resting on his thigh. She couldn't help noticing how his relaxed stance stretched the material of his slacks tautly across the hard columns of his legs.

"I don't think you understand how serious dad's situation is. It isn't just the mine he's going to lose, but his home, everything he's worked for all his life. In his condition, he can't start all over."

"I know he'll be lucky to end up with the clothes on his back." Jett took a drag of his cigarette, squinting at her through the smoke that swirled up to burn his eyes. "That's one of the things I learned when I ran a check on him. And I admired the way he underplayed how much he stood to lose, as if he had something tucked away while he was betting his last dollar. He's a proud man with a lot of class."

"You wouldn't say that if you had seen him after you left this afternoon." Glenna laced her fingers together in front of her, twisting them as she tried not to remember how he'd looked. "You broke him. I've never seen him like that— with no fight left in him—no pride. He's given up. When you left, he laid down as if he hoped he would fall asleep and die. I sat with him, trying to think of a way I could—" Her throat tightened, choking off the last of the sentence.

"That's when you got the idea to come here." His gruffness drew her glance. An agitated impatience dominated his action as he crushed his cigarette in the ashtray and set it aside.

"You were his last hope, Jett. There isn't anyone else in a position to help him." She took another step toward him, reaching out to touch his arm in an unconsciously beseeching gesture. "I accept that as a business move a merger with dad might not be that beneficial to you. But can't you reconsider his proposal on a personal level? Help him because he needs it?''

A muscle flexed in his jaw as his impenetrable gaze locked with hers. With an almost violent abruptness, he straightened from the table, moving so suddenly that one minute her hand was touching his arm and in the next there was only empty air.

''You don't know what you're asking, Glenna.'' He shook his head with an angry kind of weariness, his hand on his hips.

''He needs you,'' Glenna stood quietly in front of him. ''Explain to me what I have to say or do to make you listen to me.''

''What if I told you to take off your robe?'' His glance flicked to the satin bow with raw challenge.

Slowly she raised a hand to untie the front bow. Her fingers trembled slightly as she pulled an end of the ribbon to unfasten it. When it was untied she eased the robe from her shoulders and let the shiny material slide down her arms. Catching it with one hand before it reached the floor, she reached out to lay it on the table atop his papers. Then boldly Glenna lifted her gaze to his face.

An inner warmth kept her from feeling the coolness of the air touching her exposed skin. The matching nightgown was styled like a slip. Turquoise green lace, the same shade as the satin material, trimmed the bodice. The clinging fabric revealed the rounded shape of her breasts, her nipples appearing as small buttons beneath the material. After tapering in at the waistline, the nightgown flared gently over her hips, ending just below her knees. The lace-trimmed hemline was broken where the gown was split up the side, almost to mid thigh.

Jett was making note of each detail before he finally returned her look. The black fires leaping in his eyes ignited an answering spark in the lower half of her body, aroused by the rapacious hunger in his gaze. Glenna swayed toward him. There was a slight tremor in his hands as he reached out to loosely grip the sides of her waist.

"How can I persuade you to change your mind, Jett?" Her voice was one step away from a whisper.

Her fingers were splayed across the front of his shoulders. Beneath the material of his shirt, she could feel the tautness of his muscles, as if he was holding all his instinct in check.

"This is an appeal to the lascivious side of my nature, isn't it?" he asked as his wandering gaze noted the uneven rise and fall of her breasts beneath the lace bodice of her nightgown. "You came here tonight to convince me to help by tempting me with your body. Are you prepared to carry it through?"

His bluntness seemed to cast a sordid light on her behavior. She lowered her gaze to the unbuttoned collar of his shirt as she struggled to defend her present action. "I love my father. I can't stand by while he's being destroyed without trying to save him. It doesn't matter what I have to do in order to accomplish that."

"Why did you think you could change my mind?" His breath fanned her temples, warm and tangy with tobacco smoke, while his hands inched her closer to him.

"You once said that I tempted you. I wasn't sure whether you meant it or if it was just a line you'd used many times before," Glenna admitted on a breathless note because his mouth was nuzzling her cheek and ear.

"You're not tempting," Jett murmured, working his way to the curve of her neck. "You're irresistible. You knew exactly what would happen when you knocked on my door."

"I hoped." She tipped her head to one side, giving him more access to the sensitive areas he sought and inviting him to continue the stimulating exploration.

From the base of her throat, he nibbled up the other side of her neck. A soft moan escaped her lips as they sought the satisfaction of his kiss. His mouth hardened on hers, spreading a hot and brilliant glow through her body. The pressure of his hands increased, threatening to crack her ribs as the intensity of his need engulfed him. His tongue probed apart her lips and teeth to unite with her tongue.

Her hands slid around his neck, her fingers seeking the thickness of his lustrous black hair. A fiery heat seemed to turn her bones to liquid as the crush of his hands fitted her to his length. The sleek material of her gown was a thin barrier, blocking out none of the sensations of his hard embrace. His caressing hands made restless forays over her shoulders, back and hips, relentless in their need to touch and possess every possible inch of her.

Slowly Jett dragged his mouth from hers while raising his head no more than a breath's reach from her lips. "You know I want to make love to you." His low husky voice was a rough caress. "I can feel the way you're vibrating. You knew this was going to happen when you came; that it would ultimately come to this moment."

"Yes." Her face remained uplifted, her eyes trained on the tantalizing nearness of his mouth, her lips parted in an aching invitation for his possession.

"And your sole reason is because of your father. Would you be here now, Glenna, if I was a fat old man?" Jett mused.

"I don't know," she admitted, because she had not been presented with that situation. Jett was a virile, exciting man who desired her, and who was in a position to help her father.

"Your loyalty to your father runs deep, but I'll never believe that you would have considered using sex as a bargaining tool if I hadn't aroused you." His mouth brushed her lips as he spoke the words, claiming them at the end of the sentence.

The tidal wave of passion that flooded through her veins made it impossible for Glenna to argue with his statement. His arms shifted to scoop her off the floor and hold her cradled against his chest.

The door to a bedroom was standing ajar. Jett kicked it the rest of the way open and carried her into the lightless room. Slowly lowering her feet to the floor, he stood her up beside the bed. His hands glided up her sides, pulling her gown with them and lifting it off her head. The room was all in shadows with only a glimmer of light shining in from the sitting room as he began unbuttoning his shirt. Glenna could barely see what he was doing. A wild anticipation licked along her veins, sending tremors over her skin.

"You are going to help my father, aren't you?" That was still the motive for her presence. It was where she got her strength. Discretion would have sent her from the room, long ago.

His arms clasped her shoulders to draw her naked body to the hair-roughened bareness of his chest. Despite the dimness, his mouth found her lips and locked sensually over them. His kiss gave Glenna her answer.

"No more talking," he murmured and leaving her standing beside the bed, he began to shed his clothing.

Everything was going to be all right, thanks to Jett. Her father was not going to lose his purpose in life, his will to live. Jett was giving it all back to him. Something wet trickled down her cheekbone. Tears that had been forbidden to fall for so long were now slipping out of her eyes. It seemed right, somehow, that they were being shed in happiness.

Her arms opened to Jett now undressed, gathering his muscled torso into her embrace. Her breast swelled as his hand took its weight in his palm. A muffled groan escaped his throat before his mouth claimed her yielding lips but then he dragged his mouth from hers and stiffening, lifted his head.

"Are you crying?" His puzzled question indicated that he had tasted the saltiness of her tears on her skin.

"Yes." She smiled while her hands glided over the steel smoothness of his shoulders. Glenna knew she had to explain. "I can't help it. I'm happy. You've made everything all right again. I can see dad's face when I tell him that you have changed your mind."

There was a long silence during which Jett remained perfectly still, looking at her in the darkness. Then, with a heavy sigh, he turned away from her. "I can't help your father, Glenna." An iron thread ran through his low statement.

It gripped her by the throat, numbing her with disbelief. "What?" It was barely a whisper.

"I can't help him," Jett repeated his statement more forcefully.

All she could see was the dark silhouette of his back. "You let me believe you were going to so you could make love to me," she accused in a voice that ached with his betrayal.

"Yes, I did," he muttered tersely. "And I wish to hell that I'd kept my damned mouth shut!"

"But I thought we made a bargain." Glenna saw him bend to pick up his pants. She heard the rustle of the material as he stepped into them and zipped them up.

"I never agreed to it," he reminded her. He tossed something at her in the darkness. It landed at her feet. "You'd better put that on."

The touch of her fingers recognized the material of her nightgown. When she looked up, Jett was vanishing through the doorway into the sitting room.

CHAPTER EIGHT

HER FINGERS CURLED into the material of the gown, its silken texture contrasting with the rawness of her nerves. A desperate kind of angry confusion pushed her into action as Glenna picked up the gown and slipped it over her head. She tugged its length down over her hips and hurried after Jett.

She paused in the doorway, her gaze sweeping the sitting room to find him. Shirtless, he was standing at the table, lighting a cigarette. Glenna seethed with the knowledge of how very close he had come to tricking her.

"Why did you do it?" Her voice shook on the hoarse demand.

His dark gaze sliced to her, slashing over the provocative nightgown that covered her shapely form. With a disregard for the order of the papers stacked on the tabletop, he snatched the robe she had laid on them and lobbed it across the room to her.

"You'd better put that on, too," he snapped.

She was forced to catch it as it swirled around her middle. Jett half turned away, tense muscles rippling and flexing along the back of his shoulders as he ran a hand over his rumpled black hair. Acting out of instinct, Glenna slipped her arms into the sleeves of the robe.

"Why?" she repeated her question with the insistence of hardness.

"My God, surely you can guess!" Jett retorted with a fury that was barely contained. "Let me run through the scene for you. A sexy redhead knocks on my door in the middle of the night, dressed in a clinging negligee. When I let her in, she asks for my help. And in return, she'll go to bed with me. Since I want to go to bed with her, I take advantage of the situation— the same as any man with a normal sex drive would do."

The anger of shame scalded her. "I trusted you, but it was all a deception." Glenna choked on a bitter laugh. "God, you must have been laughing at how gullible I was!"

"If that was true, we'd be in that bedroom right now making love!" The partially smoked cigarette was crushed in the ashtray and left to smolder. With long impatient strides Jett crossed the width of the room to a credenza and opened a door to take out a decanter of Scotch and a glass. "The deception worked, but unfortunately, I couldn't go through with it."

At the moment Glenna found no consolation in that fact as she watched him splash a jigger of Scotch in the glass and bolt it down. She was too filled with degradation because she had nearly sold herself for nothing. The loss of self-respect was shattering.

"Whatever gave me the ridiculous idea that

you would agree to help my father? I should have realized what kind of man you are when you admitted you knew he would be financially ruined if you turned him down this afternoon.'' Glenna had realized, but she had been too filled with her foolishly noble purpose to notice it at the time. "You weren't interested in helping him—only yourself.''

"I *can't* help him!" Jett angrily stressed the verb, slamming the glass down on the credenza.

"Ha!" It was a scornful sound. "You *won't* help him because it doesn't suit you to do so. You can't get any bigger than Coulson Mining. I'm not an expert, but even I know that!"

"Do you think your father is the only one in the industry who suffered financial problems during that long strike a year ago?" he challenged. "Multiply his problems a hundredfold and that's what I had. My company lost money then, too, because the overhead and management went on. My stock of coal supplies was exhausted because I had contracts to deliver coal. When that ran out I had to buy coal to make the shipments, which meant paying a higher price. My firm is recovering just as your father's would have if he hadn't ran afoul of the safety regulations. I can't absorb his losses without risking my company. I can't do that. It's his life versus hundreds. Can you understand that?"

His harshness, his roughness made Glenna see how impossible it had been from the outset— how hopeless. She burned over the way he had dangled them on a string, letting them think he might save them when he knew all along he couldn't.

"It was cruel to let us think you were considering dad's proposal," she accused.

"I did consider it . . . very seriously." Jett was gritting his teeth as if suppressing the urge to retaliate with matching anger.

"Do you expect me to believe that?" she taunted. "Why would you? You've already made it clear that it was impossible from the beginning."

"Why?" He repeated her question while he began taking ominous steps in her direction, his dark eyes blazing. "I can answer that in one word—you. It has to be obvious that I'm attracted to you, that I was from the moment I met you. When I found out how much trouble your father was in, I wanted to believe there was a way I could help because I cared about you. Why the hell do you think I stayed up all night, walking and thinking and scheming?"

"You knew this morning what the answer would be, didn't you? But you made us wait all day!" Glenna was near tears again, her eyes luminous with the gray green color of storm-tossed seas. "Why didn't you put us out of our misery? Why did you drag it out?"

"If I told you this morning, what would you have done?" he challenged coldly, coming to a stop in front of her. The intimidating breadth of his naked shoulders and chest towered before her eyes. "You'd be hating me—the way you are now. The name Coulson Mining means dollar signs to you. Even now after I've explained to you, you still believe I could have helped your father. I would end up getting blamed for your father's failure. So I stole this morning. And I would have taken tonight with you. I should have. You were more than willing."

He raked her with a look that reminded Glenna just how willing she had been. She was sickened by the way she had bartered herself, and subsequently embittered that he tread on her unsuspecting nature.

"You don't have to remind me of that," she protested huskily.

"You aren't going to give me credit for telling you the truth, are you?" he declared with disgust. "I didn't carry out the deception. I could have."

"I'm amazed that you didn't." Sarcasm crept into her voice as she blindly turned away. "I can't believe how incredibly naive I was. For my father's sake I was going to give myself to you, so certain that you would appreciate my gallant gesture. But I forgot I was dealing with a ruthless magnate instead of a gentleman."

"I can't prevent your father from losing what he has, but if you need anything, Glenna—" Jett began, ignoring her insulting words.

"I'll never come to you," she flared. "I never want to hear your name again."

Because she knew it would always remind her of the way she had opened herself to humiliation. She had lowered herself—cheapened her father's name—with her foolish tactics. She could never forgive Jett, because she couldn't forgive herself.

With hot tears filling her eyes she hurried toward the door. Jett called her name, but she didn't pause. Afraid he would pursue her, she rushed down the hallway to her suite, breathing in sobs. Tears were streaming down her cheeks when she slipped inside the room and closed the door.

"Glenna? Glenna, is that you?" Her father's voice called to her from the open door to the adjoining suite.

Quickly she swallowed the sobs in her throat and wiped hurriedly at hot moisture on her cheeks. "Yes." There was a thready sound to her voice. Footsteps approached the doorway. She sniffed back some tears and tried to sound calm. "Did you want me, dad?"

"Where have you been?" The forlorn question was echoed by his expression when he appeared in the opening. "I called several times but you weren't here."

Glenna was careful not to face him directly as she turned down the covers of her bed and took her time plumping the pillows. "I'm sorry. Did you need something?" Although she tried hard to conceal it, there was a definite waver in her voice.

"Where were you?" His attention sharpened at the way she avoided his question.

Hesitating, she realized she couldn't hide the truth from him. "I went to talk to Jett," she admitted thinly. "I thought I might persuade him to change his mind."

There was an awkward silence. "In your nightclothes?"

The accusal struck a raw nerve and lifted her hurt gaze to his paling face. The tiredness and defeat became mixed with dismay.

"Yes," Glenna whispered as she began to shake with the sobs she could no longer hold back. "I'm sorry, dad, but I just couldn't stand by while you lost everything." It seemed to take him a long time to cross the room to where she stood. Intense sadness gleamed in his eyes. Quietly he studied her wretched expression.

"What happened, baby?" he asked with grim concern.

"Nothing." She shook her head in a mute kind of pain and shuddered when his arms went around her to comfort her. "He insists that he isn't in a position to help you."

"Then he didn't—" Her father paused, not needing to finish the sentence.

"No." It was a rasped answer as Glenna began to cry softly. "I wanted to make things right for you. Instead I've hurt you more, haven't I?"

He gathered her into his arms and hugged her close. "This is all my fault," he murmured.

"No. You aren't to blame." She refused to let him take that burden as she rested a wet cheek against his flannel robe. "It was all my idea. I was so desperate that I didn't stop to think how embarrassing it might be to you. On top of losing everything you have worked all your life to build, now I've let you down.''

''I'm afraid I let you down,'' he sighed heavily. ''I had given up because I thought I had lost everything in life that mattered. But I still have you, Glenna. I should have remembered that.''

She closed her eyes. ''Can we leave first thing in the morning? I can't face Jett again.''

''You were beginning to like him, weren't you?'' He drew his head back to look at her.

''I could have, if he had been different.'' But that wasn't exactly the truth. ''If circumstances had been different,'' she corrected.

He patted her gently. ''You climb into bed. Maybe tomorrow morning things won't look as bleak as they do now.'' With an arm around her shoulder, he urged her toward the bed.

''Are you all right?'' Self-consciously she wiped at the tears on her cheeks and lifted her head to study him.

''I will be,'' he promised, but he looked exceptionally tired when he smiled to reassure her.

After she was in bed he tucked the covers around her and bent stiffly to brush a kiss on her forehead. Before he left the room he turned off the light. Lying beneath the covers in the dark, Glenna thought about the episode with Jett and how much worse it could have been. He hadn't carried out the deception to its final conclusion. Her anger had been a face-saving device to salvage her pride. Knowing that did not improve Glenna's opinion of herself.

A HAND shook her awake. She groaned a protest, weighted by some sleepy depression that she didn't understand. But the hand on her shoulder was insistent that she should wake up. Finally she rolled onto her back and opened her eyes. Memory rushed back with the sunlight flooding the room. First, Jett's announcement that there would be no merger, then her father's despondency, followed by her disastrous attempt to appeal to Jett to reconsider. Pain sawed on her nerve ends.

"Good morning." Her father was standing beside her bed, smiling down at her.

Glenna blinked and tried to refocus. Her father looked so different from the man she had seen last night. He was dressed in a bright sport shirt and blue slacks. There was color in his freshly shaved cheeks and a twinkle in his eye.

"Come on. Get up," he coaxed. "It's a new day outside and I'm hungry for breakfast."

Confused, she pushed herself into a sitting position and stared at this cheerful replica of her father. Her expression drew a hearty chuckle from him. That only deepened her frown.

"What reason do you have to be so happy?" She shook her head in total bewilderment.

"Why are you so glum?" he grinned.

Her mouth opened, but all she was capable of doing was releasing a short incredulous breath. Her reasons were so obvious that there wasn't any need to list them. Helplessly she searched for some explanation for his attitude.

"How can you say that?" she said finally.

"Because I've just spent a night counting my blessings," he informed her.

"I know we have some, but... have you forgotten that we're losing the company, our home, everything?" It wasn't that she wanted him to become depressed again, but the change in his attitude was so drastic that Glenna was worried.

"And that's blessing number one," he stated with a brisk nod of his head.

"A blessing?" she echoed.

"Yes, because now we know it's a fact, so we can stop wondering and worrying whether we're going to find some way or someone to bail us out of our mess," Orin Reynolds explained as if his reasoning was perfectly logical.

"Dad, are you feeling all right?" Glenna eyed him warily.

"I'm fine. A good dose of optimism will cure what's ailing you, too. Hop out of bed and I'll give you your first injection over breakfast." He glanced at his watch. "I'll give you twenty minutes to get dressed and meet me downstairs at the restaurant."

As he moved toward the door Glenna protested, "But dad, I don't want to meet Jett again. He might be there—"

"That's blessing number two," he winked. "He's already checked out of the hotel and gone."

The vision of his beaming smile stayed with her after he had disappeared into the outer hallway. Driven by curiousity Glenna climbed out of bed. Her own low spirits had been overwhelmed by her father's ebullience. His sunny disposition was forcing her to venture out of the darkness whether she wanted to or not.

Exactly twenty minutes later she joined him in the restaurant. He'd already taken the liberty of ordering for her. She stared at his choices that were so indicative of his mood. First, a glass of orange juice—liquid sunshine—two eggs sunnyside up, a rasher of snapping-crisp bacon, and golden brown toast with orange marmalade.

"Dad, I'm not hungry enough to eat all this." Actually she wasn't hungry at all.

"You'd better eat it," he shrugged goodnaturedly. "After all, we can't be sure where our next meal is coming from."

"And you're smiling about that," Glenna accused, quickly swallowing the sip of orange juice she'd taken. "I don't understand because last night—"

"Last night I was selfishly looking at all I was losing instead of what I was gaining," her father interrupted.

"What are you gaining?" She couldn't see where there was anything. "We are going to lose our home."

"We're going to lose a *house*," he corrected with gentle patience. "It's just walls, ceilings and windows. It's too big for us and costs too much to heat. What do we need all those rooms for? And look at how many things we've accumulated over the years. We can sell twothirds of the furniture and still have enough left over to furnish a small house. What we do sell, we can call them antiques and make a handy sum.''

''But—''

''I know what you're going to say,'' her father interrupted again with a knowing smile. ''What about all the memories? Happy memories are stored in your heart, not in a house. They are something you can never lose.''

''And what about the mine?'' Unconsciously Glenna found herself eating the breakfast her father had ordered.

''Ah, yes, the mine. What a responsibility—what a burden has been lifted from my shoulders,'' Orin Reynolds sighed in contentment. ''No more worrying about payrolls, insurance, unions, contracts, taxes, regulations, deliveries, and the hundred and one other things that are part of running a business.''

''But what will you do?'' she frowned.

''Do you know what I remembered last night?'' he asked rhetorically. ''Do you know I never wanted to run the mine? But it was the family business, so when it came my time I took over for my father.''

Glenna never knew that. She had never even suspected it. ''What did you want to do?''

He paused for a minute, considering her question. A sudden gleam sparkled in his gray eyes, dancing and mischievous. Chuckling laughter flowed, its contagious amusement making Glenna smile.

''I remember when I was a teenager I always

wanted to make moonshine.'' He laughed louder. ''Maybe that's what I should do. Take what little money we get from selling the furniture and buy a patch of ground back in the hills and brew up some moonshine.''

''Dad, you can't be serious!'' She was amused, astonished, prepared to believe almost anything after the revelations of the last few minutes.

''Why not?'' His expression continued to be split by a wide grin. ''I've heard that there's still money to be made in it. If any revenuers come around, we can dress you up in a Daisy Mae outfit and you can try a little of your friendly persuasion on them. You might improve with practice.''

Her cheeks burned at his teasing reference to her attempts last night to get Jett to change his mind. She hastily lowered her gaze to her place setting.

''How can you joke about that?'' she murmured tautly.

''You've got to learn to laugh about it, Glenna.'' His voice was softly insistent, gentle in its understanding. ''What else can you do? Are you going to hide your eyes every time you think about it?''

All the logic in the world didn't make it any easier for Glenna to bear the knowledge of what she'd done. It would be a long time before she could laugh about it.

''I admit,'' he continued, ''that when you first told me, I was outraged...shocked. Then I was flattered that you cared so much for me to go to him. Flattered, and a little proud. I guess there are some people who wouldn't understand that. They would say that the best of intentions wouldn't excuse a wrong. But I don't think that is what's making you hang your head. Do you want to know what I think it is?"

He waited until Glenna asked, "What?"

"It's because you were beginning to like Jett Coulson. When he didn't accept your offer and its conditions, you felt that you had cheapened yourself in his eyes. You're afraid that if he'd look at you now he wouldn't see a lady of strong principles, but a woman who's an easy make. Am I right?"

His accuracy strangled her voice, forcing her to nod in admission. There was a fine mist of tears in her gray eyes, enhancing their greenish cast. Her father reached over to crook a finger under her chin and lift it.

"You hold your head up," he ordered with a smiling wink. "If he's so dumb that he doesn't see what you're made of, then he isn't worth your tears."

She smiled, a little tightly, but the warmth and adoration shining in her eyes wasn't forced. "How do you do it?" There was a thread of amazement in her emotionally trembling voice. "I was feeling so terrible this morning. I still hurt, but—" There was an expressive shake of her head as she paused.

"That's what fathers are for." He leaned back in his chair, a touch of smugness in his look. "To bandage up their daughters' wounded hearts and make them feel better. Clean up your plate," he admonished with paternal insistence. "We have to get packed and make the drive back. There's a lot of things that need to be done, plans to be made. Instead of sitting back waiting for things to happen it's time we started making them happen."

"You make it all sound like an adventure," Glenna murmured wryly.

"It's going to be."

It was difficult not to believe him. Glenna hadn't seen her father this carefree and lighthearted since her mother was alive. Perhaps the mine and all its problems had been too much of a burden for him. She knew it had taken its toll on his health. Without the pressure and stress of the business, he was like a new man. His mood was infectious.

CHAPTER NINE

It was late in the afternoon before they finally arrived home. The housekeeper, Hannah Burns, had evidently been watching for their return, because she was out of the front door before Glenna turned off the car motor. She came puffing down the steps to help with the luggage.

"It's about time you got here," the woman rushed the minute they were out of the car. "Don't keep me in suspense. What happened? Did you see that man Coulson?"

Her father glanced across the top of the car at Glenna. "Whatever happened to 'Welcome home?' I'd even settle for a plain 'Hello.'"

"Hello and welcome home. Now tell me what happened," the housekeeper demanded. "Was he there? Did you talk to him?"

"Yes, he was there, and yes, we talked to him." He nodded his head with each answer. "But he turned us down flat."

Hannah stared at him. Glenna could appreciate the housekeeper's confusion. How could a man look so cheerful when he had just announced—for all intents and purposes—that he was going broke?

"You're pulling my leg," she accused.

Her father assumed an expression of shocked innocence. "I haven't even laid a hand on you, Hannah. How can you say that?"

"Orin Reynolds, you know precisely what I mean," the housekeeper scolded him impatiently and turned to Glenna. She was having trouble hiding a smile as she unlocked the trunk to remove their luggage. "You tell me what happened, Glenna."

"Dad told you the truth, Hannah." There was an instant's hesitation before she added, "Mr. Coulson wasn't interested in dad's proposal."

"Would I lie about something like that, Hannah?" her father chided.

"Well, I certainly didn't expect you to be smiling about it," the woman retorted. "Don't you realize that you're going to be losing the roof over your head? Where are you going to get the money to put food on the table? Providing, of course, that you still have a table. And—"

Picking up one of the lighter suitcases, her father clamped a hand on the housekeeper's shoulder in action that indicated he was considering joining forces with her. "Hannah, you are an excellent cook. You wouldn't happen to have a recipe for a good sour mash?"

The plump woman had taken one step toward the house. She stopped abruptly at his question, her mouth opening in silent shock. Glenna wouldn't have been surprised if she had dropped one of the suitcases in her hands.

"What's the matter with this man?" She turned roundly on Glenna for an explanation. "Has he taken leave of his senses?"

"It's a long story, Hannah," Glenna laughed. "I'm sure dad will tell you all about it."

The housekeeper eyed him sternly before starting again for the house. "It'd better be good. Otherwise I'm calling a doctor. You could be having some side effects from that medicine you're taking," she grumbled.

As they reached the front door a car turned into the driveway. "It's Bruce." Glenna recognized the wagon.

She and her father waited on the stoop while the housekeeper went on inside. Bruce stopped the car beside the red Porsche and smiled a greeting as he climbed out.

"It looks like I timed it just right," he remarked noting the luggage they were carrying. "How did it go?"

"It didn't." Her father held the door open for Glenna to precede him into the house.

"I was afraid of that," Bruce replied with an I-told-you-so look and followed them into the house. "What are you going to do now?"

Setting the luggage inside the door, her father took the question seriously and didn't tease him the way he had Hannah. "Since we can no longer postpone the inevitable, we might as well start planning for it and make it as painless as possible." He led the way into the study.

"How?" Bruce raised an eyebrow and

glanced at Glenna as if expecting a protest from her, but she had been over all this with her father during the drive home.

"We can begin the necessary legal proceedings to turn the company assets over to its mortgage holders and debtors. Tomorrow I'm going to contact a real-estate company and put the house on the market." His gaze swept the room in a mental assessment of its contents. "We have a lot of furniture, household goods and miscellaneous items. We need to decide what we're going to keep so we can start selling the rest and get the best price that we can."

"But where will you go?" Bruce appeared a little dumbfounded by Orin's calmness.

"That's another thing." Her father stopped beside his desk and absently picked up a wood-carved decoy that served as a paperweight. "We need to look for a smaller place to live, maybe closer to town, although we might find a cheaper place if we stay in the country."

"What will you do without the income from the mine?" Because Bruce was well aware that a man of Orin's age with a history of heart trouble would have a difficult, if not impossible time finding work.

Glenna offered her solution to that. "Tomorrow I'm going to start making job applications. I should still be able to keep submitting freelance articles and supplement my income with writing."

"I used to be pretty good at woodworking." Her father studied the handmade decoy in his hand. "When you were younger, Glenna, I used to mess around in the workshop a lot. Remember the dollhouse I made for you and all the doll furniture?"

"There were lights in the room that you could turn on and off, operated by batteries," she recalled.

"That was enjoyable, building that." He smiled reminiscently. "It would be good therapy, too. Maybe I could set up a little shop. I have all the tools."

"Why'd you ever stop doing that?" Glenna wondered aloud.

"I don't know." He considered the question. "The business began taking more of my time, more paperwork, more problems. Then your mother died and. . . you know the rest."

"Personally I think the workshop is an excellent idea," she concluded. "What about you, Bruce?"

"Sure," he agreed with a trace of vagueness. "It sounds good."

"Is something bothering you?" her father questioned at the bewildered look on Bruce's face.

"No." There was a slightly dazed shake of his head. "I was just wondering how you came up with all these plans when you only talked to Coulson this weekend."

That drew a smile from her father. "Once you stop concentrating on keeping your head above water, it's easy to decide to swim to shore."

"I guess that's true," Bruce conceded.

"How were things at the mine while we've been gone? Did anything happen that I should know about?" It was an inquiry that was reluctantly made. Glenna could tell her father was asking because he was aware that it was still his responsibility for a while longer.

There was definitely relief in his face when Bruce shook his head. "No, it's just been routine."

"Good." He nodded and began turning the decoy in his hand, inspecting it absently. Coming to a decision, he set the wooden duck down. "I think I'll walk out to the garage and see what kind of shape my tools are in." He was halfway across the room before it occurred to him that he was deserting his guest. "You will be staying for dinner, won't you, Bruce?"

"I'd like that, thank you, if you think there's enough to go around," Bruce accepted.

"With Hannah cooking there always is." Her father continued to the foyer. "I won't be long."

Alone in the parlor-turned-study with Bruce, Glenna wandered to the fireplace. In the last few minutes she had caught herself making unfavorable comparisons between Bruce and the more dynamic Jett. One puzzle had been solved. At last she understood why she hadn't been inclined to let her relationship with Bruce develop into a more serious one. Despite all his good qualities, and Bruce had his share, there was a vital ingredient missing from his physical chemistry. Without it there was no volatile combustion.

The knowledge convinced Glenna that her relationship with Bruce would always be a casual one, but that didn't mean she didn't care about him, or wasn't concerned about his future. She turned to look at him.

"What are you going to do, Bruce, when the mine does shut down?" He had become such a part of her life in the past three years it was difficult for Glenna to picture a time when he wouldn't be around. "Have you given any thought to it?" she asked, since he had always been convinced it was unavoidable.

"I've managed to put a little money aside. I thought I might take a couple of months off, enjoy a long vacation for a change," he smiled lazily. "I can give you and your father a hand settling into a new place, and help him set up his workshop if that's what he finally decides to do. That way I can take my time and look for a really good job instead of taking the first one that comes along."

"Will you put in your application at other mining companies?" If he accepted a position away from this immediate area, Glenna knew they would inevitably drift apart. Sooner or later, she supposed, that had to happen.

"Naturally." He moved to stand beside her and lean a hand on the fireplace mantle. "That's where my expertise and experience are."

"But is it what you want?" It had been something her father had been forced into doing. "Do you like it?"

"Like it?" Bruce repeated with a shake of his head, an ardent glow firing his eyes. "I love it."

"Doesn't it ever bother you to go down that shaft?" Glenna was curious.

"I feel at home there. In a strange way I feel safe as though I was in the womb of the earth. It's something I can't really explain," he shrugged finally. "I wouldn't want to do anything else. What made you ask that?"

"I guess because I never knew until this morning that dad never wanted to run the mine. He's been in the business all these years, but it's never been what he wanted. Yet he's struggled and fought all this time to keep it in operation." She felt it spoke highly of his dedication and sense of responsibility. "It's ironic, isn't it, that out of something bad there is good. Dad is finally free of the mine."

"It's hard to believe he's the same person I saw last week. He's a changed man," Bruce commented. "I was afraid he might take it hard. But you're right, he seems relieved and happier than I've seen him."

"I know. It's wonderful."

"You've changed, too, Glenna." His gaze narrowed slightly, as if puzzling over the difference.

"Me?" She stiffened a little, sensitive to his scrutiny, not certain what his probing gaze might discover.

"Yes. I don't know quite what it is, but you

don't seem the same. It's as if you had grown up overnight. Which is crazy," he mocked at his own statement, "because you were an adult before. You look more like a woman now."

She moved away from the fireplace to escape his astute study of her. "I'll bet you've simply forgotten what I look like in the four days since you've seen me," Glenna chided him, trying to joke her way out of the situation. "You just don't want to admit it."

Bruce laughed his denial. "I'm not likely to forget what you look like." Pushing away from the fireplace, he leisurely followed her. "I know what it is." The difference dawned on him slowly. "You look vulnerable now. Before you always seemed so confident and self-assured, capable of tackling anything."

"That's silly." Her laugh of protest was brittle.

"No, it isn't. All of this has hit you harder than it has your father," he reasoned. "That's why you look lost, and a little afraid, isn't it?"

"No—" Then Glenna realized he was offering her a logical excuse. She checked her denial to hug her arms around her waist in an unconscious gesture of self-protection. "Maybe it has," she lied.

His hands gripped her shoulders to turn her around. "You know I'll help in any way I can. You don't have to face this thing alone. I'll be with you."

When he bent to kiss her Glenna turned her head aside and his mouth encountered the coolness of her cheek instead. "Don't, Bruce." Her voice was flat as his caresses left her cold. There was no need to experiment to see how his kiss would compare with Jett's. It couldn't. Glenna stood rigid within his hold, not fighting him as she stared to the side.

"What have I done, Glenna?" He was irritated and bewildered by her rejection. "Anytime I get close to you anymore you pull away from me."

"It isn't you. It's me," she replied because it wasn't fair to let him wonder if he had done something to upset her.

Sighing heavily he let his arms drop to his side. "Do you want me to leave? I don't have to stay to dinner."

Glenna lifted her head to look at him. "I'd like your company tonight, Bruce." She tried to tactfully make him understand her view of their relationship.

"My company but not my kisses." He read between the lines.

"I'm sorry, but yes," she admitted her meaning. Her expresssion remained composed, gentle but firm.

"I guess we've got that clear." His mouth tightened grimly as he turned away and walked to an armchair. "Why don't you tell me about your weekend, then?"

"There isn't much to tell." Glenna wished he'd chosen a less disturbing topic—like the weather. "The Greenbrier is a fabulous place, but it wasn't exactly a pleasure trip."

"What was Coulson like?" His choice of subject went from bad to worse.

"Just about what you would expect—although he's difficult to describe." Which he wasn't. Black hair and eyes, hard compelling features, with a latent sexuality about him that awakened hers. "He's intelligent and self-assured. He isn't one to suffer fools gladly." She remembered that he had walked in the woods and watched the sunrise. "He has an appreciation for the serenity and beauty of nature."

"How was he to deal with?"

A wry smile broke around the edges of her mouth as she remembered his afternoon meeting with her father. "Jett is...." Glenna paused, realizing how easily his name had slipped from her, but there was no way to hide it. "A better poker player than my father."

"Jett. You were on a first-name basis with him?" Bruce raised an eyebrow.

"We saw him socially, as well. I called him Jett. He called dad Orin." Glenna shrugged and tried to make it appear an insignificant item. "There's nothing special about that."

"He's a bachelor, isn't he? Good-looking as I recall." His gaze searched her face.

"Yes." She knew she wasn't doing a very good job of appearing indifferent, but just thinking of Jett made her remember things that made her blood run warm.

"I suppose he flirted with you," he accused, jealousy simmering in his eyes.

"What does it matter?" Glenna had to take a stand somewhere or Bruce would continue to ask personal questions that she'd rather not answer. "It isn't any of your business, Bruce."

Taking a deep breath, he released it in a long sigh. "Things are changing too fast for me to keep up with."

The awkward moment following his comment was filled by the sound of footsteps in the foyer. Glenna recognized her father's tread and glanced toward the study door.

"Hannah sent me to tell you dinner is ready," he announced from the doorway. "The condemned are going to eat a hearty meal tonight. I came in through the kitchen and I think she was under the impression the local boy scout troupe was coming to dinner tonight. I hope you brought your appetite with you, Bruce."

The sandy-haired man was slow to respond. Glenna was relieved when she saw him fix a smile on his face. "When Hannah is cooking I always bring my appetite, Orin." Standing, he waited politely for Glenna to pass and followed her to the dining room where the table was set.

"What kind of shape were your tools in, dad?" She sat in her customary chair on her father's right while Bruce took the one opposite her.

"They are dirty and need oiling, but they are in good shape considering how long it's been since they were used last," he declared with a touch of complacency. "I'm going to enjoy puttering around out there again."

"Make sure you don't get overtired," she cautioned.

"I won't," he promised as the housekeeper entered the dining room carrying a green salad and four wooden bowls on a tray. Her father shifted closer to Glenna so he wouldn't be in Hannah's way as she lowered it to the table. "Glenna, do you remember where we stored your dollhouse? Was it in the attic or that back bedroom?"

"That does it!" Hannah dropped the tray on the table and whirled away. "I'm calling the doctor."

"Why?" Glenna was the first to recover "Hannah, what's wrong?"

The housekeeper paused near the kitchen door to impatiently explain. "First he comes with a lot of crazy talk about making moonshine. Now he's asking about dollhouses. He's going through his second childhood. That's what it is."

Laughter began slowly, then gathered force. Finally Orin managed to catch his breath and explained his plans to the housekeeper.

CHAPTER TEN

THE RADIO was turned on full blast, which was the only way Hannah could hear it above the vacuum cleaner. The racket was getting on Glenna's nerves. "Be patient," she told herself. Hannah was almost finished cleaning the living room.

Stretching, Glenna ran the long-handled dust mop around the top of the walls where the cobwebs invariably gathered. A faded blue bandanna was tied around her head to protect her auburn hair from the dust. A plaid shirt and brushed-denim jeans made up the rest of her work clothes.

It seemed strange to see the study empty of furniture and the fireplace mantle bare. The last load of their belongings was stacked in the foyer, waiting for her father to return with Bruce and one of his friends to take it to their new and smaller home.

Everything else had been sold. The larger items had been sold individually through advertisements in the paper. Others had been included in a garage sale. The items that were left had been taken to an auction and sold.

So she and Hannah were busy cleaning so the

new owners of the house could move in this coming weekend. And Hannah liked to listen to the radio while she cleaned. Between the radio and vacuum cleaner, Glenna could barely hear herself think.

"Glory be! Glenna!" Hannah shouted from the living room. "Come in here!"

The strident summons sent Glenna racing to the living room, certain some disaster had occurred. From the doorway everything appeared all right. The housekeeper was over by the window with the vacuum cleaner and the portable radio was blaring on the floor near Glenna's feet.

"What is it?" Glenna shouted. Hannah answered her. At least Glenna saw her mouth moving and heard pieces of words above the din of the radio and the vacuum cleaner, but not enough for it to make sense. Losing her patience she demanded, "Will you turn something off? I can't hear you."

As she reached down to switch off the radio, the housekeeper turned off the vacuum cleaner. The sudden silence was heavenly to Glenna. She could even hear herself sigh.

"There's a helicopter out there in that cleared patch of field by the driveway," Hannah announced and motioned for Glenna to come to the window and see.

"A helicopter?" She took a step toward the window.

"It's mine." A man's voice spoke behind her. Not any man's voice, but Jett's.

Glenna pivoted to find him standing inside the opened front door. A pair of mirror-dark sunglasses hid his eyes from her, but there was no mistaking him. The sleeves of his white shirt were rolled up the length of the cuffs and he was wearing dark slacks. His coal-black hair was windblown into a careless order.

After the initial shock was over, the blood rushed through her veins. Two months had not dimmed her memory of him nor lessened the impact he made on her. The longing to erase that one night when she had lost his respect gnawed at her like a cancer.

"I knocked, but with all the noise no one heard me," he explained.

"I'm sorry." Glenna found her voice, thin though it was. "But as you can see, we were busy cleaning." She loosened her grip on the dust mop. It moved slightly as if to illustrate her explanation.

Hannah came forward to draw attention to her presence, which had been virtually ignored by both Glenna and Jett. She stopped beside Glenna to study the man the helicopter had brought.

"Hannah, this is Jett Coulson...of Coulson Mining." She added the last in case the housekeeper didn't immediately make the connection. "Hannah Burns is...has been...our housekeeper for years."

After today it would be the past tense. Hannah was starting a new job as a restaurant cook, which Glenna's father thought was appropriate since she was inclined to cook for large numbers.

The introduction was acknowledged by twin nods. Hannah was plainly curious, eyeing him warily while she tried to decide what he wanted. The mirrored sunglasses made Jett's reaction even more unreadable.

"Was your helicopter forced down?" What a cruel twist fate had made if he had reentered her life by accident.

"No. We landed quite safely," he replied in lazy assurance.

"Why are you here?" Glenna felt herself becoming nervous, crazy little quivers running over her skin.

"I came to see you." It was a simple statement.

But Glenna made it quite complicated because she didn't know if it was "you" in the singular or the plural. "My father should be back shortly."

"I said—" Jett paused to take off his sunglasses and slide them in the pocket of his shirt, turning his dark eyes fully on her "—that I came to see you."

She caught her breath, not certain what he meant by that, or why. Her poise was holding, but it was becoming brittle. She lifted her chin a little higher, needing the pride that she had cast aside the night she'd gone to him.

"What is it you want?" she asked smoothly.

"I want to talk to *you*." The emphasis implied he wanted a private discussion alone with her.

Glenna darted a glance at the housekeeper who had unwittingly provided her with the moral support of her presence. No one but her father knew of that night. If that's what Jett wished to discuss, she had no choice but to send Hannah away.

"Why don't you finish packing those boxes in the kitchen, Hannah?" she asked, knowing full well there was nothing in the kitchen to be packed. Before Hannah could remind her of that, she silenced her with a look.

With a sniff of disapproval Hannah turned on her heel and stalked to the kitchen. Her gaze wavered when she tried to meet Jett's again. His was moving over her, making Glenna conscious of her appearance. Her hand reached up to remove the bandanna from her head. She combed her fingers through the weight of her hair, raking the rich chestnut curls as she turned aside.

"You said you wanted to talk to me," she reminded him.

"Coulson Mining has negotiated a contract to operate the Reynolds Mine. I wanted to tell you before you heard it from some other source."

"Congratulations. You got the mine after all!" Glenna hadn't said it with bitterness, but the connotation was there just the same.

"I hoped you wouldn't resent it." The grimness of resignation laced his voice, drawing her glance to the quiet study of his eyes.

"I can't see that it matters how I feel about it." She lifted her shoulders in an uncaring shrug.

"It matters," Jett said with calm insistence. "This contract is business."

"I never thought for a minute that it was anything else," Glenna replied. "You explained quite clearly two months ago that it would be more economical for you to obtain the mine after dad lost it. This management agreement certainly proves it."

His hand caught her arm, holding her but not turning her. "After all this time, don't you understand yet?" There was an urgency to his low demand. Heat spread from his hand through her system, scorching nerves that had not fully healed from the last time. "I did what I had to do, Glenna."

Without making it look too obvious that she needed to escape his touch, she extricated her arm from beneath his hand. "The best thing that happened to us was when you turned down my father's proposal for a merger. We don't hold your decision against you, Jett.'

"Don't you?" His tone was skeptical.

"That's difficult to believe, isn't it?" She faced him, summoning all her pride and composure. From somewhere Glenna found a faint smile. "You should see my father now that he's free from the burden of the mine. He'll be here shortly. We've sold this house to move into a smaller place."

He glanced around the room, emptied of furniture and all signs of habitation. There was a rigid line to his jaw. "You said you would lose your home."

"It's too big, and the upkeep was too high, anyway." She repeated her father's statement concerning the loss.

"What are you going to do?" His gaze was back to her, boring and intense.

"I have a job at a printing company. Naturally I'll keep on writing in my spare time." The last thing Glenna wanted was his pity so she was quick to paint an attractive picture of their new life. "Dad is going to have a workshop where he can make toys—dollhouses, rocking horses and the like."

"You don't appear to have a problem in the world," Jett observed dryly.

"We have problems, but we're managing very well," Glenna replied. "The situation didn't turn out to be the disaster we thought it would be."

"So you no longer need or want my help?" It was a challenging statement that Glenna mentally shied from because she needed and wanted a lot of things from him, but his help wasn't one of them.

"As I told you, we're getting along just fine." Which she had been up to this moment.

"What if I said your father could have his same position at the mine again, with fewer responsibilities?" He leaned a hand against the inner door frame, his dark head tipped to one side.

"I don't think he'd be interested, but you'd have to ask him." Her tension was building under the strain of his nearness. She could feel the threads of control threatening to snap. "I'm sure he would appreciate the gesture, though."

"It isn't a gesture. It's a serious offer." His reply was curt although his expression remained steadily impassive. "It wasn't his lack of skill or competence as a manager that shut down the mine, but a series of outside influences that were beyond his control. He knows the miners, the working conditions, and the potential of the mine. We both can benefit from his experience and knowledge."

"I know you never do anything out of the goodness of your heart." Irritation crept into her reply because Jett always seemed to gain something from whatever he did.

"Don't I?"

The mask dropped from his features, but the flaring anger was merely an offshoot of the smoldering intensity of his gaze. Glenna started to turn away from its desirous message. His hands snaked out to stop her and force her to face him.

"Have you forgotten that I let you go when I could have made love to you?" Jett demanded. "Don't you remember that night? You were willing. I could have taken you but I didn't because I couldn't let you go on believing that I would help your father in return for the pleasure of your body...a body that I wanted so desperately." His voice had dropped to a hoarse whisper. "If that wasn't the right thing to do—the good thing—what was? Was I wrong to let you go?"

"No." With her head turned away from him, she stared sightlessly at a bare corner of the room. The blood was thundering in her ears and her hands rested lightly against his middle, ready to stiffen if he tried to pull her closer. "I don't want to talk about that night. I want to forget it."

"I haven't been able to forget it any more than you have." His hand tunneled under her hair and lifted aside its weight to expose the curve of her neck. He bent his head to run his mouth along it, reexploring old territory with familiar ease. "I have dreams about it at night," Jett murmured with his lips moving against her skin and his breath caressing sensitive areas.

Glenna closed her eyes to try to shut out the wild sensations licking through her veins, but it only started her head spinning. She tried to interfere with his nuzzling by turning her head into him and lifting a shoulder to deny him access to her neck. The effectiveness of her action was negated when Jett transferred his attention to the edge of her cheekbone near her temple.

"In my dreams my mind became filled with the perfume of your body." Jett continued talking against her skin, leaving male-rough kisses to punctuate his sentences. "I could feel the roundness of your breasts in my hands and hear the sweet seduction of your voice whispering in my ear. I'd wake up hungry for the taste of your lips."

"Don't." Her breath was coming in tiny gasps of tormented pleasure.

His hands were sliding down her shoulders and spine, applying pressure to bring her closer. Her forearms remained stiff in resistance, but her elbows started bending, forcing her hands up the muscled flatness of his stomach to the rock-ribbed wall of his chest.

"Why did you have to come here?" Glenna protested weakly.

"I stayed away as long as I could." Jett dragged his mouth over her lips, his warm breath mingling intimately with hers. "I wanted to give you time to get over the hurt. You don't know how I dreaded telling you and Orin that I was powerless to help. I didn't want to be the one to put that forsaken look in your eyes."

His strong teeth took gentle love bites of her lips, separating them. She was defenseless against this form of attack. Her fingers curled into the material of his shirt, clinging to it to avoid clinging to him.

"When I turned the merger down, I still had hope that I could keep you out of it. I thought if I made it clear that it was strictly business that I could later persuade you to keep on seeing me," he continued while his hands impelled her hips to rest against the powerful columns of his thighs, turning her bones to water. "Then you came to my room late that night."

"Please, I don't want to remember." She tried to elude his mouth, but it followed her.

"I knew that as soon as you realized your attempt to change my mind was hopeless, you would be sickened by what you were doing." His accurate assessment of her reaction drew a gasp from her throat. "And I knew you wouldn't want to face me after that. That's when I decided that if I was going to lose you, I was going to have that evening to remember... until I realized how much you would hate me for it. I couldn't risk that no matter how much I wanted you. I haven't stopped wanting you, Glenna."

She was helplessly confused by his uncanny perception of her behavior. Drawing her head back, she tried to wade through her dazed senses to study him.

"But how could you know that was how I felt?" This was what she didn't understand.

"You can't successfully run a company the size of mine without knowing what motivates people," Jett explained, letting the short distance remain between them while the compelling possession of his gaze roamed over her face. "I had a chance to find out a little bit about you as a person before that night. I wasn't wrong in my conclusion, was I?"

"No," Glenna admitted with aching relief.

It required no encouragement to persuade her to meet him halfway. His demanding kiss exorcised the guilt from her conscience and replaced it with self-respect. With her worth restored, she could meet him on common ground again. There was no longer any need to hide her face from him. Jett wouldn't have permitted it if she had tried, and Glenna didn't try. There was too much wondrous rapture to be found in his kiss.

"I want to keep on seeing you." His voice was muffled against her throat.

"I want to see you, too," she whispered, because she didn't ever want to stop seeing him. The certainty of that knowledge left her a little giddy.

Jett lifted his head and ran a hand over her cheek before tangling his fingers in the thick mane of her hair. "Where are you moving? How far is it from here?"

The trembling roughness of his voice and the implied possession of his touch convinced Glenna that Jett was equally disturbed by her nearness. It gave her a fleeting sensation of power.

"The new house is only a few miles away," she told him.

The velvet blackness of his gaze became shadowed by a raw regret. "Do you know how impossible it is for me to commute back and forth between here and Huntington even with a helicopter at my disposal? My schedule fills a sixteen-hour day. I would barely arrive here before it was time to leave."

"I know." Glenna felt his frustration ripping through her, leaving behind an awareness of how precious each moment was.

"Move to the city," he urged. "At least there we can spend more time together and I won't be wasting so much traveling time to and from. You don't need to worry about work. I have some connections at one of the newspapers. I can arrange for you to be hired as a reporter."

"It isn't that easy," She shook her head in a reluctant protest. "We've signed a year's lease on the house. Besides, dad wants to live in the country. I can't walk off and leave him, not in his condition. Don't ask me to do something like that, Jett."

"I'm not going to be content to see you only a couple of times a month, Glenna," he warned. "It's been too long now."

Glenna agreed wholeheartedly with the last, but she was plagued by a sense of lost time. "Why didn't you come sooner? You should have told me how you felt before now instead of letting me imagine what you were thinking," she protested.

"You wouldn't have believed me. You were too caught up in your own self-guilt to listen," Jett replied wisely.

"It's been such an agonizing two months," she admitted and traced the outline of his cheek with her fingertips. "If it hadn't been for Bruce and dad, I think I would have crawled in a hole and buried myself."

A muscle flexed along his jaw, tightening its line with grimness. His attention shifted to a lock of curling auburn hair, the hardness of regret darkening his eyes. Glenna swayed toward him, needing the reassurance of his kiss that everything was all right now.

The slamming of the front door stopped her while the sound of her father's voice reversed her direction out of Jett's arms. "Fred is backing the pickup truck to the door so we can load these boxes, Bruce. Did you ask Glenna about that helicopter outside?"

As she turned toward the doorway to the foyer, she saw Bruce frozen within its framework. His very stillness indicated that he had been standing there for several seconds, if not several minutes. Glenna could tell by the numbed look of disbelief in his face that he had seen and heard enough to know what had been going on prior to his arrival. The atmosphere in the room became electric when his gaze met Jett's in silent confrontation.

Her father's appearance on the scene kept it from becoming volatile. Glenna was standing freely beside Jett when her father paused in the doorway. The instant he saw Jett a broad smile spread across his face.

"Jett!" He greeted him with obvious delight and came striding across the room, a picture of health. "What brings you here? I saw the helicopter outside, but I didn't get a good look at the insignia."

"You're definitely looking better, Orin," Jett shook hands with him.

"Thank you, Jett. I'm feeling better, too," her father stated with a decisive nod, then turned to invite the third man to participate in the conversation. "Bruce, come here. I want you to meet Jett Coulson. Bruce Hawkins was my engineer and manager at the mine," he explained to Jett.

Bruce walked stiff-legged across the room like a challenger about to do battle. "I've heard a great deal about you, Mr. Coulson." He measured him with a firm handshake.

"Orin has mentioned to me what an asset you were to him," Jett returned as he sized the sandy-haired man up with' a sweeping look. Neither made a reference to Glenna. Yet, when the introduction was over, Bruce assumed a protective position at her side.

In the interim her father ran a quick eye over Glenna. Astutely he noted the glowing flush in her cheeks and the kiss-swollen softness of her lips despite the slightly uncomfortable atmosphere that prevailed.

"What brings you here, Jett?" her father questioned with a smile of benign interest. "Is this a social call or business?"

"A little of both," Jett admitted, sending a glance at Glenna to indicate the social side of his visit. "I stopped by to let you know we've negotiated a contract to manage your mine."

"My ex-mine," her father corrected without bitterness. "Congratulations. I'm glad to hear it's going to be in competent hands. When will you be reopening it?"

"Soon. Naturally we'll have to make the necessary changes to pass the safety inspection before we can go into production. But first I want to find myself a good man to put in charge." Jett took a cigarette from his pack and lighted it, studying her father over the flame. "You immediately came to mind. Would you be interested?"

"Oh, no, you don't!" her father laughed. "I just got that elephant off my back."

"I would like you to seriously consider it," Jett persisted. "The responsibilities would be considerably fewer this time around. You have all the qualifications and experience I'm looking for, plus a knowledge of this particular mine's characteristics."

"I'm flattered that you should offer me the position, but I'm not interested," her father refused as Glenna had guessed he would. "But if that's what you're looking for, Bruce fits the description. He may be a little shy on the experience side, but I'd recommend him. I happen to know he's looking for a position that would keep him in this same general area. Isn't that right, Bruce?"

Before he answered Bruce slid a look at Glenna. The glance confirmed she was the reason he didn't want to move away. It was a message no one in the group missed, including Jett. Glenna felt the penetrating study of his gaze. At this point she couldn't reassure Jett that her relationship with Bruce was still very platonic, on her part.

"That's true, sir," Bruce replied to her father's question.

"Would you be interested in the job?" Jett inquired in that brisk yet smooth business tone Glenna knew so well.

"I might be." Bruce didn't reject it. "It would depend on the terms of employment."

"Come by the mine office tomorrow morning at ten and ask for Dan Stockard. I'll tell him to expect you," Jett stated.

"I'll be there," Bruce nodded, committing himself to no more than a job interview.

A knock at the front door interrupted the conversation. "I'll answer it," her father volunteered. "It's probably Fred checking to see if we're ready to load the boxes."

But it was the copter pilot instead. "Sorry, Mr. Coulson," he apologized for his intrusion. "But we're already going to be ten minutes late for your next meeting. I thought I should remind you."

Impatience rippled through Jett's expression before he moved toward the foyer. "I'm ready to leave." He paused to let his gaze encompass the three of them. "Goodbye." But he looked directly at Glenna when he said, "I'll see you."

"Take care," she murmured and was warmed by the silent promise of his words and the brief flash of his smile.

As Jett left by the front door his departure carried her to the doorway opening to the foyer. Glenna was only half-aware that Bruce followed her until her side vision noticed him standing by her elbow. Self-consciously she turned her head to meet his look.

"It was more than just a mild flirtation that weekend, wasn't it?" His question didn't expect an answer, and the faint rise of color in her cheeks was the only one he needed. He moved past Glenna to the door where Jett had just exited the house. "I'll see if Fred is ready to load this stuff," he mumbled.

When the door closed behind him, her father raised an eyebrow and sent her a wry smile. "It sounds like Bruce walked in on a private moment."

"You could say that," Glenna agreed and listened to the sound of the helicopter taking off.

"In that case would it be fair to assume that you and Jett have straightened out your problems?" The knowing glint in his eyes twinkled at her.

"I think we have," she admitted, then eyed him suspiciously. "But why did you make that remark to Jett about Bruce?"

"You mean about Bruce wanting to find a job in the area? It's true," he shrugged.

"Yes, but you implied it was because he wanted to be near me. You know very well that Bruce and I are just friends," she reminded him. "But you deliberately planted a different idea in Jett's mind."

"I can't help the conclusion he reached," her father asserted his innocence with a beaming smile. "Besides, it won't hurt Jett to wonder whether he might have a little competition."

"Dad," she sighed and shook her head.

A voice echoed through the empty rooms of the house. "Can I come out of the kitchen now?" Hannah called with terse impatience.

"Hannah. I forgot her," Glenna realized with a laughing gasp. The statement immediately demanded an explanation, which Glenna made. Her father found it all very amusing, but the housekeeper's sense of humor didn't match his when she arrived on the scene.

BY THE END OF THE WEEK Glenna still hadn't completely settled into their new house. Except for the day they had actually moved she had worked the rest of the week, which left the bulk of the unpacking to be done in the evenings.

After the Friday evening meal she was in the kitchen unpacking the boxes containing the good china and crystal that had been among their family's possessions for generations. They had been among the few things they had not sold.

Glenna was on her knees unwrapping the tissue from the dinner plates when someone knocked at the back screen door. A lingering sunset silhouetted the figure outside, but she recognized him at a glance.

"Come in, Bruce," she called without getting up.

"I saw Orin out at the workshop. He's like a kid with a new toy," he remarked as he entered the kitchen.

"He spends nearly all his time out there," she agreed.

"Do you want some help with this?" Bruce knelt down beside her.

"Sure." Glenna handed him a plate with its tissue-paper covering.

Bruce unwrapped it and added it to the stack on the counter, announcing almost casually, "I start work Monday morning at the mine." Outside of that one remark he'd made when Jett had left, Bruce hadn't referred to him since.

Glenna sat back on her heels to look at him. "They offered you the position of manager."

"Yes."

"And you accepted it?"

"Yes."

"Why?" That question was too blunt. She quickly tempered it with an explanation. "I thought you were going to take a couple months off before starting another job."

"I discovered I had too much idle time on my hands with no way to pass it. Plus, the offer was a good one." He concentrated on his task, not looking up as he named his reasons. "And I liked the idea of going back to your father's mine. I feel as though I left a job half done and I need to finish it. Are you sorry I accepted it?"

"No." Glenna shook her head, auburn hair swaying at the movement. "As long as you didn't take it for the wrong reason." Which was to stay near her.

"I don't think I did."

With the last of the dinner plates out of the box, Glenna stood up and positioned the step stool in front of the cupboard. Climbing it, she opened the door to the top shelf where the china was being stored.

"Would you hand me the plates, Bruce?" She half turned to take the plates he passed up to her a few at a time. The phone rang when he gave her the last. "Will you answer it? It's probably for dad."

"Sure." Bruce walked to the extension phone on the wall. "Reynolds residence, this is Bruce Hawkins. Yes, just a moment." As she climbed down the step stool, he extended the receiver toward her. "It's for you. Jett Coulson."

Her heart flipped over, and her hand was unsteady as she reached for the phone. "Hello?" Glenna had been half expecting to hear from him before the weekend, but now that the moment had arrived, she was disturbed by it.

"Hello. I guess I don't need to ask whether you have company." There was a thin thread of grimness in his tone.

"No." She couldn't elaborate, not with Bruce able to overhear her side of the conversation. He was kneeling beside the box on the kitchen floor, unpacking the china sauce dishes.

"Did I interrupt anything?" His question was slightly challenging.

"No. I was unpacking the last of the boxes, trying to get the last of our things put away," Glenna explained. The suspicion of jealousy in his voice was a little gratifying even if it was unjustified. At this point it was a difficult thing to let him know.

"Did Hawkins tell you he's going to work for my company?"

"Yes."

"You aren't very talkative," Jett accused. "What's wrong? Is he listening?"

"Yes." She wound her fingers in the coil of the telephone cord.

"In that case I might as well come straight to the point," he sighed with a trace of disgust. "I can't get away this weekend to see you."

"Oh." That one small word was filled with disappointment.

"I have no doubt that Hawkins will do his best to keep you entertained," he inserted dryly and continued without giving Glenna a chance to comment. "I should be able to adjust my schedule to have an afternoon and evening free one day next week. I should know by Monday afternoon whether it will be Wednesday or Thursday. I'll call you then."

"Don't forget I work until four-thirty," she reminded him.

"I'll pick you up after work."

"All right."

"I'll talk to you Monday. Hopefully there won't be anyone listening then and you'll be more communicative." It was a clipped statement that betrayed his impatience. "Goodbye, Glenna."

"Goodbye, Jett." She waited until she heard the disconnecting click on his end of the line before she hung up the receiver. When she turned, Bruce was quietly studying her.

"Are you in love with him, Glenna?" he asked.

She hesitated, then rubbed her arms, remembering how it felt when Jett touched her. "Yes, I think so," she admitted on a warmly confident note.

"Is he in love with you?" was Bruce's next question.

That required a more cautious answer. "I don't know. I'm not sure." Glenna bit at her lower lip, positive that it couldn't all be one-sided. "I think so."

Bruce straightened and walked to the step stool. "Where do you want these sauce dishes? On the same shelf with the plates?" The subject was changed, not to be raised again by him.

CHAPTER ELEVEN

ON MONDAY, Glenna left the printing office early to make some deliveries for the company on her way home. Although she knew most of the customers where she stopped, she didn't stay to chat. Jett had said he would call her today. She wanted no delays that might make her miss the phone call.

That was the reason for the gleam in her gray green eyes and the smile that hovered on her lips. Even the mountain air seemed electric with anticipation as she turned into the driveway. She wasn't quite used to the small home where she lived, but it was the last thought in her mind when she stopped the car.

The slamming of her car door coincided with a ringing of the telephone in the house. Certain it was Jett, Glenna raced for the front door only to hear the telephone cut off in mid ring as her father answered it. Still she hurried into the house, breathless yet radiant.

"Is that—" She never completed the question, silenced by the sharply raised hand of her father and the stern white look in his expression.

Glenna only heard him make one response to

the caller on the phone before he hung up, and that was a clipped, "I'll be there immediately."

"What is it? What's wrong?" She read all sorts of dire things in his expression. "Has something happened?"

He measured her with an even look as he moved into action, taking her arm and steering her back toward the front door. "There's been a cave-in at the mine. That was Bidwell on the phone." He opened the door and ushered her outside.

"Bidwell." Glenna remembered he had been one of the foremen on the shifts. Evidently he'd been rehired. A single line creased her forehead as she dug the car keys out of her purse again. "Why did he call instead of Bruce? Was anybody hurt?"

"They think there are six men trapped." He left her and walked around to the passenger's side of the car while Glenna slid behind the wheel.

"Oh, no." His statement stopped the hand that started to insert the key in the ignition. On the heels of her alarm came another more frightening thought. "Bruce?"

"He's one of the men believed trapped." It was a simple statement not designed to spare her.

Its bluntness caught at her breath, squeezing her lungs until she wanted to cry out. Her rounded eyes sought her father. Neither had to say the things that were silently understood. Bruce could be trapped or buried under a rubble of rock. He could have escaped harm or be seriously injured. He could be with the others or isolated from them. Yet her father's calm strength reached out to invisibly steady her, and prevent any panic from letting her imagination run riot.

"Was there an explosion?" Her hand trembled as she succeeded in inserting the key in the ignition. "Fire?"

"No fire." He relieved one of her fears. "Bidwell was outside the entrance and said he felt the ground vibrate, then heard the rumbling inside the mine and saw the coal dust belch from the opening."

Glenna started the car and reversed out of the driveway, picturing the scene in her mind and feeling the terrible dread that must have swept through the workers on top. She blocked it out because she knew it would give rise to panic. She concentrated on her driving, suddenly impatient with the twisting mountain roads that denied speed.

"When did it happen?" she broke the chilling silence that had descended on the car.

"About twenty minutes or so before Bidwell called me," her father answered. "He notified the main office first, then called me."

Even though her father had no more to do with the mine, Glenna understood the reasoning. This was a close-knit community. In a time of crisis everybody helped. When miners were trapped, every mining man in the area volunteered his services. With her father's intimate knowledge of the mine and experience, he was an obvious choice to be notified in the event of an emergency.

Time was the enemy. It ticked away as Glenna drove as fast as she dared. She wondered if the word had reached Jett. Surely it had by now. Bruce, and the men trapped with him, had to know that every available resource was being galvanized to effect their rescue. If they were still alive. A chill went through her bones, making her shudder.

On the last mile to the mine Glenna encountered other traffic headed for the same destination. News of the cave-in had traveled fast through the West Virginia hills. Others were already arriving on the scene when she turned the car into the parking lot.

Leaving the car parked alongside others, Glenna hurried with her father toward the fence gate. There was already a hubbub of milling people outside the mine buildings and entrance. They were an assortment of miners, families, and townspeople.

A small wiry man separated himself from the group to meet her father. Glenna recognized him as Carl Bidwell, the foreman who had called her father with news of the accident.

"Am I ever glad to see you, Mr. Reynolds," he declared.

The man's face was pale and etched with lines of stress and worry. Glenna knew her face showed the same brittle tension marked with latent fear as the faces of all those around her.

Her gaze sought the mine entrance, but the steadily growing crowd of people blocked it from her view. Bruce was somewhere inside that mountain. Glenna clung to the belief that he was still alive. He had to be.

"Has anything developed since you called me?" her father questioned. "Have you made contact with any of those inside?"

The negative shake of Bidwell's head was in answer to both questions. As others in the milling crowd recognized Orin Reynolds they pressed forward, besieging him with questions he hadn't had a chance to ask for himself.

The chopping whir of a helicopter interrupted the conversation, drowning out the voices as it approached. All eyes turned to it. Glenna recognized the Coulson Mining insignia on its side. Coming in low over the heads of the crowd, it whipped up a wind that swirled dust clouds through the air. Turning her head aside, Glenna shielded her eyes from the blowing particles of dirt with her hand and tried to keep the dark copper length of her hair from blowing in her face.

It landed on a helicopter pad within the fenced area around the mine, kicking up more dust to obscure the vision of those on the ground. Three men in business suits emerged from the chopper and crouched low to avoid the whirling blades as they hurried toward the crowd. The minute they were clear, the helicopter lifted off.

With a profound sense of relief, Glenna recognized Jett as one of the three men. Just the sight of his sun-bronzed craggy features gave her strength. Once free of the overhead threat of the chopper blades, he straightened his tall frame and let long strides carry him to the knotted group of onlookers. A hand reached up to absently restore some order to the untamed thickness of his black hair.

The concentration of concern had darkened his eyes to an ebony pitch. Glenna felt the penetration of his gaze the instant he singled her out from the crowd. He altered his course slightly to approach her, but it was to her father that he spoke.

"I'm glad you're here, Orin." He grasped her father's hand, the edges of his mouth lifting in a grim semblance of a smile.

"Bidwell phoned me," her father replied.

"We can use your help," Jett stated.

"I'll help any way I can. Even if you hadn't asked, I would have been here. Like the others—" her father's glance encompassed the crowd of people gathered at the site "—waiting to lend a hand if needed."

"What's the status?" Jett made a search of the encircling ring of people. "Where is Hawkins?"

Someone on the outer edge answered, "He was in the mine when it collapsed."

Jett's gaze swerved sharply to Glenna, revealing his ignorance until that moment of the fact that Bruce was one of the missing men. His piercing look seemed to question while it reached out to comfort. Tears sprang into her eyes and her chin began quivering. Desperately she wanted to have his arms around her and ward off the chill of uncertainty with his warmth. But it was impossible and improper in this mob of people.

Something flickered across his expression, a raw frustration mixed with a savage kind of anger. Then a poker mask covered his features and his gaze was withdrawn from her. This was the time for cold clear thinking—not emotions.

"Let's go to the office." At his clipped statement the milling crowd separated to form a corridor through which Jett walked toward the mine buildings. Bidwell, the two men from the helicopter, Glenna and her father followed him. Jett continued issuing directives as he walked. "I want to see a diagram of the mine. I want to know the location of the collapse and the approximate location of the men inside when it happened."

Glenna swallowed the lump in her throat and blinked away all the tears but one that trembled on the edge of her lashes. It she brushed away. Her father's arm was around her shoulders, silently offering her support and comfort as they followed Jett and the others into the building.

"How many men were inside? Eight?" Jett shot the question at Bidwell.

"We thought it was eight, but we accounted for two men. It looks like there are only six in-

side, sir," the wiry man replied, intimidated by
the presence of the head of the firm.

Jett paused in an outer office. "Do you have
their names?"

"Yes, sir."

"Have all their families been notified?"

"All except two, sir. We haven't been able to
reach them yet."

Until that moment when Jett swung around to
face her, Glenna hadn't believed he knew she
had followed him inside. His eyes made an im-
personal inspection of her. "Are you all right?"
he asked flatly.

She knew he was really asking if she was in
control of herself. "Yes," she assured him.

"Would you get the names of the two men
from Bidwell and take the responsibility of
making certain their families are notified?" It
was an unpleasant task he was offering her, but
it showed his belief in her ability to handle it.

"I will." Glenna quietly assumed the role he
had given her.

While Jett, her father, and the other two men
went to the inner office, Bidwell remained
behind to give her the names before joining
them. Both families knew Glenna through her
father. It took her the better part of an hour
before she was able to locate both of them and
break the news to them with a woman's compas-
sion.

Even when that job was done a sense of responsibility remained with her, a desire to do
something that might in some small way help.

She emptied the morning black dregs from the large coffee urn and made fresh coffee. That would be needed and more before all this was over.

All the while there was a hum of activity around her. Directives came from the private office where Jett had set up his headquarters. And reports flowed back in. The crowd outside grew larger with friends and relatives of the trapped men as well as the multitude of volunteers. Naturally the press arrived, first newspaper reporters and later on television crews.

Cleve Ross, one of the men who had arrived with Jett, emerged from the privacy of the inner office to issue a statement to the news media. It dealt in specifics, pinpointing the location of the cave-in on a diagram and the possible location of the men inside when it happened. Although the extent of the collapse wasn't known, the statement held out hope that the men were behind the wall of rock and dirt. The report actually contained little that Glenna hadn't already known.

Afterward she and two office workers volunteered to answer the incessantly ringing telephones and respond to the endless inquiries regarding the fate of the trapped miners. It kept Glenna occupied, even if it didn't allow her thoughts to stray from the worry over Bruce and his companions.

By half-past seven Glenna had stopped paying attention to who came and went through the door to the yard. As she replaced the telephone receiver on its cradle she heard the griping tone of a familiar voice behind her and turned in the swivel chair to recognize the plump figure of their former housekeeper, Hannah Burns.

"I can't stand here holding this forever," she was complaining, a large foil-mounded baking sheet in her hands. "Someone will have to clear a table to set this on."

Directly behind her there were two high-school-aged girls carrying similar pans, and a boy holding a large commercial coffee urn. A shirt-sleeved man was hurrying to clear space on a long worktable.

"Hannah." Glenna ignored the ring of the phone to rise quickly to cross the room. "What are you doing here?"

"I knew you and your father would be here," the woman replied with a brief glance. "I figured nobody would be thinking about their stomachs at a time like this. So I took it upon myself to do it for them. I brought some cold sandwiches, salads, and chips. A couple of the grocers donated the food and these young people volunteered to help fix it."

She set the baking sheet down and folded back the aluminum foil to reveal the stacks of sandwiches, then motioned the two girls to set their trays beside hers. The boy found a place for the coffee urn beside the one Glenna had fixed.

"Go get the rest of the things from the car,"

Hannah ordered and her trio of helpers set off to obey.

"You're right, Hannah," Glenna admitted. "No one has thought about eating. I'm glad you did."

The practicality of the woman had a steadying influence on Glenna. Her mere presence offered support, and the comfort of someone who had weathered many a crisis with Glenna before.

"We certainly aren't going to feed the entire mob of gawkers out there, but the men's families and the workers are going to need some nourishment before this is over. People always have more hope when hunger isn't gnawing at them," Hannah philosophized.

The remark made Glenna aware that the hollow feeling inside might be filled by some food. The three teenagers returned with sacks of chips, paper plates and cups, as well as huge bowls of potato salad. Glenna helped them arrange the assortment of food into a buffet. When word spread there was food in the building, there was an influx of hungry people with the alternating shifts of rescue workers always having priority at the table.

A security man who had worked for her father and been rehired by Coulson approached Glenna. She knew the man only as Red, although his hair had long ago thinned and turned gray.

"Miss Reynolds," he addressed her respectfully, removing his cap. A deeply etched worry shadowed his pale eyes. "There's a Mrs. Cummins out there with two small children. Her husband is one of the men in the mine. I tried to get her to come in and eat, but she refused. She just sits out there with the little ones huddled around her, starin' at the entrance to the mine. Maybe if you spoke to her, she'd listen."

"I'll see," she promised.

Leaving the security guard she paused to tell Hannah where she would be in case she was needed and went outside in search of the woman. Local sheriff's deputies had joined the company's security force to cordon off the area around the mine entrance and separate the sightseers from those directly associated with the situation.

Glenna had no difficulty spotting the woman the guard had described. She was standing away from the others, a four-year-old pressing close to her legs, a two-year-old in her arms, and her protruding figure indicated a baby on the way. Twilight was pulling a dark curtain over the mountainscape but floodlights made the fenced yard around the mine and its buildings bright as day. Glenna crossed the lighted space to the woman and her children.

As she drew closer she heard the four-year-old boy whimpering, "I want to go home, mommy. I'm hungry."

"No. We can't go 'til daddy comes," the woman replied as if repeating it by rote, her attention not straying from the mine.

"Mrs. Cummins." Glenna saw the ashen

strain on the woman's face as she half turned in answer to her name, reluctantly letting her gaze waver. "I am Glenna Reynolds."

The surname immediately drew a response. "Have you heard something?" the woman rushed. Glenna was shocked to realize the woman was no older than herself, but worry had aged her with haggard lines. "Tom? Is he—"

"I'm sorry. There hasn't been any news," Glenna explained quickly to check the outpouring of wasted questions. "It might be a while before we know anything. We have sandwiches and hot coffee inside. Why don't you come in and have something to eat? You'll feel better.'

"No." The woman had already lost interest in her. "I'm not hungry."

"Maybe you aren't, but you have to think of the children and the baby you're carrying," Glenna insisted, but the woman indifferently shook her head.

The little boy tugged at his mother's skirts and repeated, "I'm hungry." He didn't understand what was going on, or the silence of all the others in the crowd that was broken only by the murmur of hushed voices.

"If you won't come in," Glenna persisted, "would it be all right if I brought out some sandwiches for the little ones?" The woman hesitated, then nodded an absent agreement. But Glenna wasn't satisfied. She hated leaving the woman alone like this. "Is there someone I could call to wait with you? Family or friends?"

"No." The woman shook her head and protectively hugged the little girl tighter in her arms, a hand reaching out to touch the little boy at her side in silent reassurance. "All our kin is in Kentucky. Tom...." Her voice broke slightly. "Tom just got enough money saved to send for us last week."

"I see," Glenna murmured inadequately. "I'll bring some food for the children, and a hot cup of coffee for you."

Her remark didn't receive a response and Glenna turned away. As she started to recross the yard another woman called to her. It was the wife of one of the miners who had escaped the collapse.

"Miss Reynolds, is Mrs. Cummins all right?" she questioned anxiously. "The poor thing doesn't know a soul here."

"She's frightened." *As we all are,* Glenna thought as she allowed herself a moment to fear for Bruce. "I'm going to bring out something for them to eat. Would you stay with her until I come back? It has to be difficult being so alone."

"Of course, I will." The older woman agreed quickly to the suggestion.

When Glenna reentered the building she went straight to the buffet table of food and fixed two plates for the children. She added more than they could eat in hopes their mother would eat what was left.

Walking to the coffee urn she noticed Jett standing not far from it, deep in conversation with two other men. His suit jacket and tie were gone and his sleeves were rolled short of his elbows. Lines of sober concern were cut into his features, his dark eyes narrowed with concentration. Glenna wished she could go to him, touch him and ease some of the burden he carried, but it was just as impossible now as it had been that afternoon.

She filled a paper cup with hot coffee, unaware that Jett glanced at her, his gaze reaching out for her. She juggled the plates until she could carry them and the cup, too, then returned outside.

When she approached with the food Mrs. Cummins sat the small children cross-legged on the ground. They acted starved, hardly waiting to be given the plates before snatching the sandwich halves to begin eating. Glenna offered the cup of coffee to Mrs. Cummins.

"No. I don't want anything," she refused irritably.

Mrs. Digby, the miner's wife who had been standing silently by, pursed her lips in temper. "Miss Reynolds was thoughtful enough to bring you the coffee. The least you can do is thank her."

"I'm sorry. All I can think about is Tom," the woman began in a frightened kind of explanation.

"All you can think about is yourself," Mrs. Digby criticized.

"Please," Glenna didn't think Mrs. Digby was handling the situation properly.

But the miner's wife paid no attention to her. "Do you think you're the only one whose man is in there? Miss Reynolds has a man in there— Bruce Hawkins—and you don't see her standing around feeling sorry for herself. She's trying to help. You have two little babies here and look who is making sure they have something to eat."

When Glenna saw that the woman's words had shocked Mrs. Cummins into an awareness of her children, she understood the woman's tactics. When soft words failed, a figurative slap in the face usually worked. It was now.

"Is it true?" Mrs. Cummins searched Glenna's face, seeing someone else's plight other than just her own. "Is your man really in there, too?"

"Yes." It was a small deceit. After all, she did truly care about Bruce even if "her man" was too strong a description. "He is." There was no harm in a white lie.

"I'm sorry. I didn't know." She reached for the coffee Glenna had brought. "Thank you... for everything."

"It's all right." When she handed her the cup, she noticed a fourth long shadow intruding on the ones they cast. She turned to see Jett standing to one side, and pivoted to take a step toward him. A question leaped into her eyes as she scanned the impenetrable mask of his features, but a brief shake of his head told her there was no news.

"I came out for some fresh air," he said in explanation of his presence.

Taking a cigarette from his shirt pocket, he bent his head to the flame of his lighter. Glenna took the last few steps to be closer to him. She found it difficult to talk; all her thoughts were overshadowed by the knowledge that men were trapped in the mountain beneath them. It almost seemed wrong that her pulse should quicken because she was near him.

"The accident happened when they were installing an air duct to make it safer to work in the mine," she murmured. "There's a certain irony in that."

She knew instantly that she had chosen the wrong subject. She could almost see Jett shut her the rest of the way out. If he had sought her out, as she suspected, it had been to escape talk of the accident and the rescue efforts.

"Jett." She didn't know how to reach him so she turned away instead. "Hannah may need me. I'd better go in."

He said nothing when she walked away.

CHAPTER TWELVE

TWENTY MINUTES LATER Jett entered the building and went directly to the private office, never glancing Glenna's way. She squared her shoulders and helped the plump housekeeper rearrange the buffet table into a snack counter. A few stragglers came in to eat some of the remaining sandwiches.

At half-past ten her father came out of the private office and stopped to pass on the message, "Jett wants some coffee. Take him a sandwich, too," he added. "He hasn't eaten anything."

"I will," she said as he continued on his way to the washrooms.

With a cup of coffee balanced on the sturdy paper plate, she knocked on the inner office door. There was a curt response, granting her permission to enter. Jett barely glanced up when she entered, seated at his desk and bent over an array of papers and diagrams.

"I brought you some coffee and something to eat," Glenna said and set it down on a small cleared space on the desk top. She discovered there was no one else in the room as he reached for the coffee, but showed no interest in the sandwich. "You need something. Dad said you haven't eaten."

Her voice seemed to make no impression on him, his concentration not wavering from the papers he was studying. Jett took a sip of the coffee and set it back down to lean an elbow on the desk and rub a hand across his mouth and chin.

"That's where they've got to be if they are alive," he declared aloud, his jaw hardening. A wave of grim exasperation broke over him. "Dammit, right in the bowels of the mountain!"

"Bruce called it a womb," Glenna remembered, this time claiming Jett's attention. She was drawn to the window that overlooked the mine yard, its dusty panes creating a haze. "He said he felt safe inside it, safe and protected. I know he isn't afraid, and that helps me."

The squeak of the swivel chair told her Jett had risen. "I promise you it won't be his tomb, Glenna." He came to stand beside her by the window. "I'll get him out of there."

She lifted her gaze to him, a smile touching her mouth. "I know you will." She knew it as surely as she knew her own name. Some powerful force seemed to flow between them in that moment—until Jett shut it off by looking out the window. Disappointed, yet knowing this was not the appropriate time to press a personal issue, she glanced at his desk and the untouched sandwich. "Is there anything I can get you? Anything you want, Jett?"

His head turned to slide her a hard and hungry glance. "I want you, Glenna." He reached out to possessively take her hand and draw her toward him. His gaze ran roughly over her face. "I want what *you* can give me. What *only* you can give me."

She didn't know what he meant, but when his mouth moved hungrily onto hers, she gave him the only thing she possessed—all of her love. It flowed from the wild singing of her heart, a searing rapture that knew no end.

Yet there was something desperate in his need, something raw and aching that a single kiss couldn't satisfy. His hands were all over her—stroking, feeling, caressing yet never able to get their fill of her. Through it all her senses clamored with the desires he aroused. They quivered through her every nerve end like concentric circles in a pond, each ripple as perfect and delightful as the first.

A knock on the door she had left ajar brought the embrace to an abrupt end. Before the shutters fell to block out his expression, Glenna saw the glitter of wildness in his eyes and was shaken by the force of it.

His broad shoulders and back blocked her from the view of the interloper. Jett turned his head to the side, but didn't turn around to see who it was.

"What is it?" he snapped over his shoulder.

"There's a phone call on line two...about that equipment—you wanted to know whether it was available or not," was the answer.

Glenna heard the sigh rip through him, heavy and long. The grip of his fingers loosened on her arms, gradually letting her go altogether. "All right. I'll take it." He left her to walk to the desk and pick up the phone, punching the second button for the incoming call. "Yes."

Their moment of privacy was gone. The present situation had reclaimed its priority. Glenna slipped quietly out of the room, inwardly radiant with the emotions Jett had aroused yet confused by his attitude.

The embrace seemed to have left her with a keener perception because she immediately noticed the tiredness in her father's face, something that had escaped her notice only moments before. He was on his way into the office so it was natural for their paths to meet as she was coming out.

"Are you all right, dad?" Her concern was instant.

"I'm fine," he insisted, but on a weary note.

"Don't overdo it," Glenna warned. "Get some rest. Isn't it enough that I have to keep wondering about Bruce? Don't make me start worrying about you, too."

"Glenna is right." Jett's voice came from a few feet behind her. He had the coffee cup she had brought him in his hand. "Sack out on the couch, Orin, and get some rest. I'll wake you if anything develops. I want that ambulance outside used for the men in the mine, not you."

Her father glanced at the green vinyl couch in

the outer office. "Maybe I'll lie down for a little while," he conceded to his tiredness.

"The equipment?" Glenna referred to the phone call he'd taken before she left.

"It's on its way." He left the office, walking past her. "The coffee is cold." Jett walked to the long table and poured a fresh cup from the urn. Someone came in and immediately sought out Jett to make a report. Within a few minutes he was surrounded by people. Glenna walked to a desk to take up a post answering the telephones.

Around midnight the activity slackened. The strain and the late hour began to take their toll on Glenna. She found a straight-backed chair in a quiet corner and settled onto it, resting her head against the wall. It wasn't long before she dozed off. She had a wonderful dream. Jett was carrying her in his arms again, and putting her in his bed, lightly kissing her.

The first gray light of dawn wakened her, but her senses were slow to leave behind the dream. The aromatic scent of Jett's after-shave and the pungent blend of tobacco mixed to make the smell that belonged uniquely to him. With her eyes closed she could feel the rich fabric of his suit jacket against her cheek, the texture of it and the scent of him surrounding her. It was several seconds before she realized she was lying down, not seated in the chair propped against the wall.

Glenna opened her eyes slowly. She was on the couch in the private office. His suit jacket was folded to make a pillow for her head. It hadn't been a dream. Jett had carried her in here and laid her down, slipping off her shoes and leaving the sensation of a soft kiss to linger on her lips.

"Good morning." Jett was standing beside his desk, leaning on it while several others, her father among them, studied papers spread in front of them. Jett was half turned to watch her, but the others only glanced her way. His face was haggard and drawn from no sleep, a dark stubble of beard shadowing the lean hollows of his cheeks, but a slow smile spread across his mouth. A warm reckless gleam was in his ebony eyes, catching at her heart.

"Better have some coffee," he advised.

"Yes," she murmured and sat up, wiping the sleep from her face. He sent him a secret smile left over from her dream. She sobered quickly as she remembered the reason they were all gathered in this place. "Is there any news?"

The special look was erased from his expression, replaced with a cool aloofness. "No. Nothing." Jett turned his back on her, focussing his attention on the quiet discussion of the other men.

Sighing over the loss of that brief intimacy Glenna rose and went to the washroom in the outer area to freshen up. No one had made fresh coffee since late last night, so she put on a fresh pot. By the time it had finished Hannah arrived. This time she brought pans of homemade sweet rolls, still warm from the oven.

Whether it was the aroma of hot rolls or freshly perked coffee, or simply the starting of a new day, a crowd of people invaded the building. Workers, families, and members of the news media arrived to learn the progress that had been made during the night, if any.

Before the rolls and coffee were gone, Glenna fixed a large tray to carry to the men closeted in the inner office. Her appearance broke up the discussion under way, especially when they saw what she brought.

While she was passing out the coffee and rolls, one of Jett's advisers said, "The reporters are going to want a press conference, an update on our progress. We won't be able to put them off for long."

"Schedule it for seven o'clock." Jett rubbed a hand over his beard and glanced around the room. "Does anybody have a razor?"

A razor was found as well as a clean shirt. The outer office was transformed into a make-shift conference room, complete with television lights and microphone stands. Glenna sat back in a corner of the large room where she was out of the way of the proceedings.

Promptly at seven Jett came out of the office accompanied by three other men. The first was in work-stained clothes, the man physically superintending the rescue efforts. The other two were the key advisers Jett had brought with him. These three read the prepared statements and fielded the questions from the reporters while Jett remained in the background.

At the very last a reporter put a question directly to him. "Mr. Coulson, would you explain why you are personally directing this rescue? Don't you have any qualified people working for you who could handle the operation?"

Jett moved to the microphones, but before he responded to the question, Glenna saw his gaze seek her out in the far corner of the room. "The three men with me are very highly qualified and extremely capable. They have answered your technical and, sometimes, very pointed questions for the past twenty minutes. I believe that proves their ability."

"But you didn't answer my question," the reporter reminded him.

"No, I didn't answer it," Jett agreed with a taunting half-smile. "Because if I was in Huntington, you would ask why I was there when six men are trapped in one of my mines." His barbed retort brought a moment of silence to the room. He glanced around it and announced, "That's all the questions for now."

Jett and the other three men shouldered their way through the crush of reporters trying to have one last question answered before they disappeared into the private office, but their clamoring voices were ignored. It was a full quarter of an hour before the bulk of the news media gathered their gear and left.

An hour later things had returned to normal—at least as normal as they had been the night before, with telephones endlessly ringing and people forever coming in and out of the building. Glenna wasn't sure the exact minute the atmosphere changed, but it started as a thin thread of excitement flowing in from outside.

Everyone seemed to notice at the same moment that the voices of the waiting people seemed louder with a certain cheerfulness in the sound. The building buzzed with questions. From a window someone saw the rescue operation's superintendent crossing the yard to the building. The word instantly flashed that he was smiling. It brought everyone to their feet and the men out of the inner office.

Unconsciously Glenna gravitated to Jett's side, afraid to anticipate the news yet silently doing so. When the door opened to the man, a white smile was showing in his coal-dusted face.

"They're alive," he announced. "The second unit punched into an unblocked air shaft and made contact."

Cheers went up around her, but Glenna dug her fingers into Jett's forearm, needing his strength and support. "How many?" she asked the all-important question.

"Six. All six of them!" he confirmed. "Hawkins said there was one broken leg, but the only other injuries were minor bruises."

She went weak with relief and turned into Jett, hugging her arms around his waist and burying her head against his chest. "Thank God. Thank God," was all she could whisper. She felt the answering tightness of his arms around her and the pressure of his cheek against her hair. Then his hands slid to her shoulders to push her from him. She looked up, beaming with the good news. "They're alive," Glenna repeated under his probing gaze.

His hands moved to pull her arms from around him and hold her hands in front of him, but when Jett spoke it was to quiet everyone. "Let's save the celebration until we have them out of there." A sobered chorus of agreement followed his suggestion. "When will that be, Frank?" he asked the man.

"Hell, we'll make it by noon!" the man declared on a decisive note of optimism.

"Don't take any chances," Jett cautioned. "Do it safely."

"Yes, sir."

"There's still work to do." Jett broke up the party, sending them back to their individual duties. Glenna received a brief glance before he let her go to return to his office with his select group.

With the uncertainty removed, the atmosphere in the building was much lighter. People talked louder, joked, and found more reasons to laugh. The high spirits were infectious.

Most of the four hours passed swiftly, then dragged at the last when it started to stretch into five. As the moment of final success drew closer everyone was outside waiting for the moment when the rescued miners emerged. Jett was one of the last to come out, but he didn't join Glenna standing with her father on the fringe of the anxious families.

Two ambulance attendants waited close to the mine entrance with a stretcher for the one injured miner with the broken leg. It was one of them with a closer view who raised the shout, "They're coming!"

As expected the injured man was first, carried in the saddle of two men's arms. Glenna stretched on tiptoe for a glimpse of Bruce, wanting to see for herself that he was safe and unharmed. He was one of the last to come out.

With all the other families hurrying forward to greet their menfolk, it seemed the natural thing for Glenna to do the same. A wide but tired smile spread across Bruce's face when he saw her approach. He dragged off the hard miner's hat and narrowed his eyes against the bright sunlight.

Laughing and crying at the same time, Glenna ignored his coal-blackened clothes to hug him, not caring that the dust on his cheeks rubbed off onto hers. There were so many voices, she couldn't hear hers or his above the others. When Bruce kissed her, she kissed him back. But when his mouth hardened to demand passion, she stiffened in resistance and drew away. A troubled light entered her eyes, making them more gray than green. Bruce probed her expression, his smile fading.

"I'm glad you're safe, Bruce. I—"

"You don't have to say anything." He shook his head to check her explanation and loosened the arms that held her. "It's all right." His gaze drifted beyond her to scan the crowd, stopping once on a target. Then he took her hand, turning her around. "Come on."

He laced his fingers with hers so she was walking beside him. It was several steps before she realized he had a specific destination, and that destination was Jett. She felt the piercing stab of Jett's gaze knife into her, but he turned away before they reached him.

"Coulson!" Bruce called out to stop him.

Glenna was stunned by the harsh and savage light that glittered in Jett's sidelong glance. "I got him out for you, Glenna." His voice was a low angry sound. "Don't ask for more than that."

She was shaken by the suppressed violence that rumbled through his voice. His features were set in rock-hard lines, but there was no mask to conceal the bitter rage under their expressionless surface.

Jett's reaction only made Bruce smile with a wry twist of his mouth. He took Glenna's hand and extended it to Jett. "I believe she belongs to you," Bruce said as calmly as if he was returning lost property.

There was a puzzled flash in Jett's expression. After a second's hesitation, he reached out to claim her hand. His frowning gaze sharply locked with hers to probe deeply into the recesses of her soul. Neither seemed to notice when Bruce moved away.

"Is it true what he said?" There was an uncertain quality in his voice that Glenna had never heard before. "Do you belong to me?"

The smile that broke on her face was one of vague disbelief. "I've always belonged to you... since that night I came to your room... probably even before that," she admitted.

His fingers tightened on her hand, nearly crushing the delicate bones. "Last night I heard you admit to those women that Hawkins was your man."

"I agreed because it made Mrs. Cummins feel less alone in her fears," Glenna explained earnestly. "And I did care about Bruce, but as a good friend. I already told you that. Surely you didn't believe I had changed my mind."

"It happens," Jett said, towering closer. "When a woman has taken a man for granted a long time, she can suddenly realize how much he means to her when he's in danger."

"It didn't happen," she assured him.

"It could have. Hawkins was there when you needed him. I wasn't. He helped you through the rough times when I couldn't." His fingertips stroked her cheek in a caress that bordered on reverence. "When I saw how worried you were about him, I was determined to get him out of that mine. I couldn't let you down again, even if it meant you wanted him instead of me."

"It's you I love, Jett." Glenna swayed toward him.

Violent tremors ran through him as he gathered her into the crush of his arms and began smothering her face with rough kisses. In that moment she was convinced of the depth of his feelings for her and a wild joy raced through her blood.

"Marry me, Glenna. I don't want to lose you." The words came in a raw whisper from his throat. "Never let me lose you again."

"Never," she breathed into his descending mouth.

PAMELA BROWNING

... is fireworks on the green at the Fourth of July and prayers said around the Thanksgiving table. It is the dream of freedom realized in thousands of small towns across this great nation.

But mostly, the Heartland is its people. People who care about and help one another. People who cherish traditional values and give to their children the greatest gift, the gift of love.

American Romance presents HEARTLAND, an emotional trilogy about people whose memories, hopes and dreams are bound up in the acres they farm.

HEARTLAND ... the story of America.

Don't miss these heartfelt stories: American Romance #237 SIMPLE GIFTS (March), #241 FLY AWAY (April), and #245 HARVEST HOME (May).

HRT-1

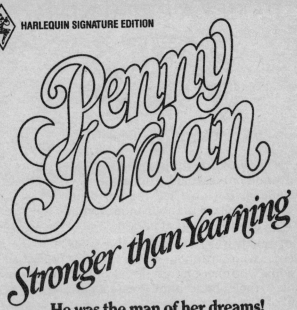

Penny Jordan

Stronger than Yearning

He was the man of her dreams!

The same dark hair, the same mocking eyes; it was as if the Regency rake of the portrait, the seducer of Jenna's dream, had come to life. Jenna, believing the last of the Deverils dead, was determined to buy the great old Yorkshire Hall—to claim it for her daughter, Lucy, and put to rest some of the painful memories of Lucy's birth. She had no way of knowing that a direct descendant of the black sheep Deveril even existed—or that James Allingham and his own powerful yearnings would disrupt her plan entirely.

Penny Jordan's first Harlequin Signature Edition *Love's Choices* was an outstanding success. Penny Jordan has written more than 40 best-selling titles—more than 4 million copies sold.

Now, be sure to buy her latest bestseller, *Stronger Than Yearning*. Available wherever paperbacks are sold—in June.

STRONG-1R